W9-CBR-532

BLIND SPRING RAMBLER

Also by John Douglas:

Shawnee Alley Fire

BLIND SPRING RAMBLER

a novel

by

JOHN DOUGLAS

ST. MARTIN'S PRESS
NEW YORK

 For information, address St. Martin's Press, 175 Fifth Avenue, New York, N.Y. 10010.

Library of Congress Cataloging-in-Publication Data

Douglas, John.
Blind spring rambler / John Douglas.
p. cm.
ISBN 0-312-02167-4
I. Title.
PS3554.08257B57 1988
813'.54—dc19 88-12020

First Edition

10 9 8 7 6 5 4 3 2 1

for Seb & Steven

It's always night, or we wouldn't need light.

—Thelonious Monk

1

We made it to Washington just in time for the long layover. Our train wasn't listed on the board to leave until after mid night.

I was still young then. In awe of being in the Nation's Capitol. Excited about what lay ahead of us. Squirming to get going.

To kill time, we hit the hot streets. When we tired of hiking the hard pavement, Grant and I ate in a greasy spoon of a place, and then it was back to Union Station, where Grant bought a *Washington Star.* He sat on a bench reading it while I sat next to him gazing down at the heavy book I'd lugged all day. I was too keyed up to concentrate on the words.

The porters, ticket agents, and other station workers were all abuzz about the President's visit earlier that Wednesday. They chattered about the Secret Service men and about the private train with its presidential coach, *Superb.*

"Damn," I said, "if we'd only gotten here a couple hours earlier, we could have laid eyes on the President himself."

I'd not yet seen a living, breathing Chief Executive, though Warren G. Harding wouldn't be living and breathing much longer.

Grant stared at me over his *Star*. "If we'd gotten here earlier, we'd only have to wait longer." He tilted the newspaper's front page toward me. "Here's what Harding looks like, in case you've forgot."

"I'd like to have seen him in person," I said.

"Hell, it wasn't exactly like he stood in line, bought his own ticket, and chatted with the citizenry. Warren Harding wanted to get out of town. He wants to be far away on the West Coast, bound for Alaska, before the Senate decides to make a full-scale investigation of the Teapot Dome mess. Albert Fall's already resigned."

"Albert Fall?"

"Albert B. Fall, Harding's Secretary of the Interior," explained Grant, like he was speaking to an imbecile. "I keep telling you, Bill. If you intend to stay in this business long, you'd better watch the headlines."

Truth was, I didn't know how long I wanted to stay in the detective business, and weeks went by when I didn't so much as glance at a sheet of newsprint. I did know the Teapot Dome tangle had something to do with Elk Hills, which had something to do with federal leases on Western land, which had something to do with big oil men, who had something to do with President Harding and his cabinet. I didn't understand why I had to know more, or why I had to care.

Hell, I didn't even completely understand why we were on our way to West Virginia.

A few days earlier, Grant had come over to my corner and announced, "Pack a trunk's worth. Plan to be gone a while. We'll be leaving Wednesday." Dropping a thick red book on my desk, he'd added, "Read this."

"Why?" I'd asked. I'd felt a little like I'd been thrown back into the university classroom I'd left behind in midterm.

"We need a cover. That's your job. I've got too much else to worry about."

"A cover?"

"A reason to be in town. We don't want them to know what we're really after."

"What *are* we really after?"

His brown eyes had seemed to screw deep into his face. "We've been hired. You don't need to know more right now. I want you to sniff with a clear nose."

"Where are we going?"

"Blind Spring, West Virginia."

"You been there before?"

"Goddamn, they sure taught you in college to ask questions."

Then he'd lit a cigarette and gone out the door, leaving me with few answers. Nor had I been able to get much out of him since, except for the fact that he'd never been to Blind Spring, West Virginia, either. "But I've been to towns like it," he'd said, as if to assure me there was nothing to worry about.

Glancing over at him reading his *Star* on the station bench, I realized I didn't even know why he'd picked me as his accomplice. Certainly I hadn't performed any heroics in my first weeks on the job, nothing to attract the attention of Frank Grant, who was considered the sharpest and toughest of the agency's detectives. Could be he'd simply taken pity on me and wanted to get me out of the cluttered office and into the pristine mud where I could show whatever worth I had. Then again, could be he'd only wanted me along for "cover."

Suddenly, my thoughts were derailed by hubbub in Union Station. A group of men had rolled in, and they were yelling at each other. Their drunken voices ricocheted off the station's cathedral ceiling and walls. One guy roughly slid a case at the shins of another, who slammed it right back. It looked like an instrument case. Each of the half dozen men had one. It didn't take an experienced detective to deduce they were a band, a hot jazz band in transit.

Soon a young woman walked across the station and joined

them. Their singer, if that's what she was, couldn't have been older than twenty-one. Her high heels clattered against the marble floor as she flitted from one musician to the other. Someone finally gave her the cigarette she dearly wanted.

My mother would certainly have disapproved, but I couldn't take my eyes off her. I'd hoped to meet some pretty women on this job. The detectives in magazine stories always did.

She put the cigarette between her red lips and leaned forward so one of the musicians could light it for her. I could hear the jangle of her bracelet as she reached up to take the thing from her mouth. Then she sprawled across a bench, apart from the rest of the band. She was wearing one of those new short skirts with an uneven hem, and you could see the white of her thigh above her rolled silk stockings as she crossed her legs.

When Grant and I went to our train a few minutes later, the singer was still stretched appealingly across the bench, and the musicians were still as rowdy as ever.

The Shawnee–Potomac passenger car was nearly empty. Only a handful of people were taking the night train into the mountains. I grabbed a window seat and stared out the glass as we began to move. Grant paid no attention. Perhaps he'd been through Washington too many times.

Any train that pulled into Union Station had to back out. Strange and awkward, this backing through a maze of track. Electric, telegraph, and telephone lines formed a black road map against the continent of smoky sky above us. An engine passed us in the opposite direction, causing me a moment of seasickness. The passengers on the other train, only yards away, sat bolt upright in their lighted cars. They were nearly at their destination. We were still far from ours.

We chugged out of the District of Columbia and pressed through its thinly settled suburbs. It was a cloudy, heavy atmosphere night. Outside, the rolling Maryland fields were swallowed up by the blackness. Tearing myself away from the window, I picked up the damn book he'd assigned me and tried to read along with Grant, who seemed to be on his second trip through the newspaper. I shifted position frequently, trying to get comfortable. Several times, I closed my eyes, then opened them again to look out the window at the impenetrable blackness.

At some point during the night, the conductor walked through the car calling out the next stop. After it sounded, and felt, like we were slowing down as we rumbled over a trestle bridge, I saw a sign: HARPERS FERRY, WEST VIRGINIA.

"I thought you told me we wouldn't be there until morning," I said to Grant.

He lowered his paper. "Hell, this is just the tip of the state. If you could flatten out the damn mountains, West Virginia would be as big as one of those Western states that Harding's running to. We've got hours of rough going ahead of us. This train's a local, and we'll be stopping at small towns all night. Harpers Ferry is John Brown country, you know. You must remember it from your schoolbooks."

History, I'd found, was one of Grant's favorite topics. The whole trip from New York to Washington, he'd monologued about the Erie Railroad wars of the 1870s. I wasn't sure of his exact age, but he couldn't have even been born in the 1870s. Yet, for some reason, the back-room dealings of the New York financiers were on his mind. I just didn't understand why they were supposed to be on mine. At the same time, I hated to admit that I didn't recall the entire John Brown/Harpers Ferry saga, so I reached into some crevice of my brain and tried to retrieve what I could.

"This must be where John Brown attempted to incite a slave revolt before the Civil War," I recited. "They say he was a madman."

"No madder than anyone else following his conscience," said Grant as we began moving again.

"You sound like you know a lot about West Virginia," I said.

"Enough to get by. Just be happy we're rolling. The last time I was through these parts, the train ground to a halt between here and Martinsburg. A rail strike had been called for midnight, and the crew just strolled away, leaving the engine running and the passengers stranded. I had to hitch a canal boat west to Shawnee and hire a horse the rest of the way."

"What case were you on that time?"

"Another murder."

"A murder? Don't you think you should have told me we're working on a murder case?"

"Wouldn't you have come?" he asked, lifting the newspaper back in front of his face. "Looks like it could be an all New York World Series again, unless the St. Louis Browns steal it from the Yankees."

I was disappointed he'd changed the subject, but tried to keep him talking. "Don't rule out Ty Cobb and the Tigers. Cobb hit over four hundred last year."

"Cobb's getting old," said Grant. Then he fell silent. His outpourings of words always seemed to be counterbalanced by long silences. You could never tell what he'd say, or if he'd say anything at all.

I peered out the window again. By some mysterious zigzagging route, we kept plugging into the mountains. On a number of occasions we crossed bridges back into western Maryland, then returned over the Potomac River to West Virginia.

Finally, I gave sleep another try.

No dice. My sliding into sleep wasn't as simple as Ty Cobb sliding into second. The fact was, I just wasn't spikes-up Ty Cobb, the idol of my boyhood. And even if Grant was right, even if Cobb was getting old, he could still slice up a second baseman pretty good.

I was feeling more than ever like that wary second baseman, unsure of what was about to happen.

As the night dragged on, it seemed as if every time I neared Dreamland, the train would lurch to a stop at some small-town platform, and the land would slide, and my cheek would roll against the hard glass, or something would happen, and I would be spiked back to the present.

To the middle of a June night.

June 20—no, it had become June 21, 1923.

Shawnee–Potomac westbound.

On a mission that was being kept secret from me.

In my twenty-first year.

On my way to Blind Spring, West Virginia, a place I'd never heard of until a few days earlier.

2

We were out in the Badlands on the trail of a dangerous killer. Just who the outlaw was, or how many notches he had on his gun, I didn't know. But I did know one thing. Every time I looked up, I saw the Indians scouting us from the surrounding bluffs.

Grant shook me awake. "Coffee time."

"We almost there?"

"About an hour to go."

"What time is it?"

"A little before seven. Come on, you'll have to settle for java. I'm not paying dining-car prices for breakfast."

He stood up, dropped his folded *Star* on the seat, and started up the aisle. I lifted the heavy book off my lap and followed him. My legs were unsteady at first, and my head felt as if I had a hangover. I had no idea how much sleep I'd managed, but Grant looked none the worse for the night's journey. He always looked the same. Even his blue suit wasn't badly rumpled.

When I spotted the men's room door, I handed him the book and said, "You go ahead. I'll find you."

Seconds later, I was splashing cold water on my face and trying to focus on my reflection in the mirror. I noticed that my mustache was starting to grow in decently. I'd started the thing shortly after I'd gotten the job, imagining it would make me seem older, tougher, more mature. Add character or something. All the movie heroes had mustaches.

But I still didn't look like a hero. I looked pale, like I'd been cooped up in a city office. The brown mustache hairs stood out against my untanned skin. Maybe it was the harsh light in the toilet, but I'd never seen myself looking so pale. Maybe I was nervous.

Paleface. No wonder the Indians had been after me in my dream.

My legs were more seaworthy when I stepped out of the small compartment. As I went searching for the dining car, I wondered what kind of mood Grant would be in. Would he go on about railroad wars and industrial tycoons, or would he brood silently?

It turned out he was smiling when I found him—smiling, and talking with a dark-suited man of about fifty who was sitting at a table across the aisle from him.

"Is this your student, Professor?" asked the man as I sat down.

"Yes," said Grant. "Dr. Anders Corman, meet William Edmonson."

I nodded a hello and took a wake-up sip of the coffee that was waiting for me. Outside, the densely wooded hillsides fell away from the tracks, looking almost like a jungle in the wet early green of summer. The sun hadn't quite decided whether to show its face or sleep a while longer behind a cloud.

"From what you've told me, Professor Grant, I can't say I fully understand why you and your student are going to Blind Spring," said Dr. Corman.

I looked over at the cheerful graying man. Grant had apparently suckered him with the professor/student cover. Hell, I thought I'd left the cap and gown behind months before.

"Did you ever hear of *Child's Ballads,* Doctor?" asked Grant. He picked up the thick red book from the table and handed it across the aisle to Corman.

"I can't say I have, though that means nothing. It's certainly not my field," answered Corman as he flipped through the stanza-laden pages.

"Perhaps you've heard of Cecil Sharp?" asked Grant.

Corman handed back the book. "I don't believe so."

"Sharp was an Englishman who tramped around the Southern Appalachians before the war. He found all sorts of songs that no one knew were being sung in America, in the New World. You see, many of them were ancient Scottish–English ballads that Professor F. J. Child of Harvard had collected from Britain." Grant thumped the cover of the book to emphasize his point. "We thought someone ought to do some ballad hunting hereabouts before our modern industrial age erases them."

"Sounds noble, if a bit esoteric, Professor. I have heard there are so-called folklorists who go around collecting such material."

"Well, I'm a history professor myself," said Grant. "I'm interested in the historical side of the work. Bill's the one who's made quite a study of old ballads. Together we'll collect what we can."

"Who's underwriting your summer's expedition?"

"I've made arrangements with several institutions," said Grant in a way that made it seem like the money didn't much matter. "A few scholarly articles may come of it—in some learned journals, you understand. We may find a few items to deposit in a university library. Who knows? There might even be recordings."

"Recordings?" asked Corman with surprise. "That's quite a business these days, isn't it?"

Grant nodded. Lighting a cigarette, he said, "I've been in contact with a number of companies. It seems, Doctor, that the recording business needs a constant stream of fresh material, and, of course, some of that fresh material is actually very old.

They've learned there's an audience of Southern whites who aren't much enthralled by Caruso. There's also a Negro audience for blues songs. Even sharecroppers' cabins have Victrolas these days."

"I find it odd there's such commercial interest," said Corman.

The doctor might have been skeptical, but I thought Grant had done an awfully dazzling bunkshooting job.

Grant puffed on his cigarette until smoke veiled his face. "Dr. Corman is on his way to Blind Spring, too," he said to me. "He's visiting a patient there. What was the fellow's name again, Doctor?"

"Timothy Briggs," answered Corman. "You won't have trouble remembering the name once you've been in town a day or two. He damn near owns Blind Spring. It was barely a whistle-stop before Timothy moved in."

"Huh," said Grant, like the name still meant nothing to him, "what's this Briggs do exactly?"

"For one thing, he operates the Blind Spring mines," Corman answered. "Since the war, Timothy has made a fortune. Even the soft economy of a year or two ago didn't slow him down. Of course, Timothy had money before he moved to Blind Spring. A poor man, like you or me, couldn't have done what he's done, Professor. It takes money to make money, they say. Back in Philadelphia, there were many doubters when Timothy announced his plans to build an empire in West Virginia, but, as usual, he achieved what he set out to do. Men like John D. Rockefeller, like Timothy Briggs, frequently make fortunes in out-of-the-way places like Murry County, West Virginia. He's built it up little by little. His hotel opened only last year. Before that, accommodations were rather primitive."

"The Briggs Hotel," mumbled Grant as if he'd just made the connection. "I believe we're staying there."

"I'm sure you are," said Corman. "The mangy hotel in the county seat can't compare."

"So, you're from Philadelphia, the City of Brotherly Love?" blarneyed Grant.

"Yes. I come down once or twice a year to see Timothy. He's not well, you see, and he's holed up in his hotel and won't return home for medical treatment. He says Blind Spring is his home now. I really shouldn't be talking about a patient, you understand." Corman scratched at a gray sideburn and, to let us know he'd said enough, stared down into his coffee cup, then out the dining car window.

The hills were tougher now, not thickly wooded like before. We were clipping along through a cut between two rock faces. When we emerged, I could see entire ridges naked from clear-cutting. Soon, we began to pass clusters of men working on the hillsides and along the tracks. A wagon weighted down with tree trunks circled a slope.

"It's a big operation," said Grant.

Corman looked at us. "It'll get bigger. Timothy has a ready market for timber as well as for coal. He's convinced the Shawnee–Potomac Railroad to remove an old tunnel to broaden a cut so more tracks can be added to handle the rail traffic. In his last letter, he wrote that the company's engineering people are already in town. The tunnel project will bring thousands more people to Blind Spring, at least temporarily. It's impossible now to imagine this valley as it was only five or six years ago. The dirt farmers were thrilled to sell their straggly family plots and pick up a lunch bucket and a weekly wage."

The sun chose that moment to shine, and reflected off the white canvas of dozens and dozens of tents near the tracks. Farther off, I could see crews of carpenters hammering together frame rowhouses, which stretched up the hillside to our left. For some reason, the houses appeared hastily thrown up, even rickety, despite their newness.

"How many men work for this Briggs?" asked Grant.

"You'd have to ask Timothy or his son. I'm only estimating, but I'd guess he has several thousand employees. I believe there are two major mining operations, plus continual prospecting, plus timbering, plus the hotel. There's also mine security and various other businesses. This part of the state has never seen a larger enterprise. It's difficult to simply house all the laborers."

Smoke from wood fires hazed the tent colony. Women hunched over laundry tubs and kids played on muddy trails that wound through the complex.

The doctor pointed out the window, his white finger at an angle that led our eyes up above the tents, to the mountains on the horizon. "If you're searching out old songs and folklore, Professor, you'll no doubt venture into the hills. Don't let the moonshiners catch you."

"The moonshiners?" asked Grant, apparently as unsure as I was whether Corman was serious.

"Timothy says Prohibition, for all its good intentions, has brought out the worst sort of free enterprise among the mountaineers. They guard their stills zealously. You wouldn't want to chance upon one of the cutthroats in your travels."

Grant turned to me and laughed. "When it's all spread out, it looks like a gold mine for researchers like us, Bill."

Some gold mine, I thought, still confused about our task.

The train was barely crawling when the BLIND SPRING sign went by. We came to a halt in front of a cupola-topped station, a sprawling affair that might have been built in different stages by workmen who'd apprenticed at the Tower of Babel. The doctor was probably right in suggesting no one—except Timothy Briggs himself—could have predicted how Blind Spring would take off.

Corman pulled a gold watch from his vest pocket and looked at it. "The Shawnee–Potomac Railroad runs a tight ship," he said as he rose to his feet. He smoothed out his suitcoat and trousers, then picked up his black medical bag and began walking up the aisle.

Grant tossed some money on the table, I picked up the book of ballads, and we followed the doctor.

I noticed the clumps of men as I took the first step down to the station platform.

Big angry-looking guys.

Not the kind of welcoming committee you'd hope for.

3

Grant hit the platform with the strut of a man on serious business. He barreled ahead with Dr. Corman, outwardly ignoring the guys lining the way. I took out after them, trying to show as much confidence. I wish I could say it worked, but all cockiness drained out of me when one of the big boys blocked my path.

"Name?" His thick fingers tugged at the edge of his dusty jacket. A badge glittered in my eyes.

"William Edmonson," I answered.

"Business?" His voice struck me as a drawling growl.

"What?"

"Your business, boy? Why'd you come to town?"

Damn good question, boy.

I could have sworn he had yellow eyes, and at that moment they were glued on me.

"We're folklorists," said Grant.

I hadn't even noticed he'd doubled back to rescue me.

"You're what?"

"We've come to collect old songs and stories," said Grant patiently.

"Ballads," I mumbled, holding up the thick red book so the yellow-eyed deputy could read the spine.

The deputy's hands came at me like he was reaching for my collar, but, instead of landing on me, they took the book. He turned the volume over and over, staring at it like it was foreign to him.

"You reporters?" he finally asked.

"Folklorists," repeated Grant, enunciating each syllable slowly—*folk*—and clearly—*lor*—like he was speaking to a fool—*ists*. Maybe he was.

By then, Dr. Corman had joined us. Dropping the chipper tone he'd had on the train, he entoned, "They're legitimate researchers."

"Legit researchers, huh?" the deputy said mockingly. "Who the hell are you?"

"I happen to be Timothy Briggs' physician and friend."

Corman's words were still hanging in the air when another man with a badge showed up.

"Back off, Smithers. Mr. Briggs is expecting Dr. Corman," said the new guy, who immediately sounded reasonable to me. He turned to Corman. "Excuse Smithers here, Doctor. He's new. He just got carried away. We've been ordered by Sheriff Chaney and Mr. Briggs to question anyone we don't recognize."

The second deputy—whose name turned out to be Kirk—seemed not only more reasonable but also more intelligent than the one called Smithers. At least Kirk's eyes didn't flash yellow and his voice was soft when he answered the doctor's questions.

"You've surely heard of all the labor unrest in West Virginia the last couple years," explained Kirk. "Sheriff Chaney has learned there's a union organizer on his way to Blind Spring. The troublemaker might already be in town. Or, there could be more than one of them. We've been told to send any suspicious newcomers packing. Mr. Briggs says the red scavengers needn't import labor disputes into Murry County. They aren't going to tear us apart like they tore Logan County apart in 'twenty-one."

"Timothy has told me a little about the Logan County mine

war," said Corman. "Some of those rednecks are still on trial, aren't they?"

Kirk nodded. "Charged with murder and treason."

"I don't believe you have anything to fear from Professor Grant and his young associate. I had coffee with them on the train. They're not dangerous men."

Through it all, Grant maintained one of his rock-hard silences and let Corman do the talking.

Down the platform, I could see groups of deputies interrogating other people who'd climbed off the morning train. They were actually frisking one guy. A woman was standing next to him and, even from a distance, I could sense her fear. The man being frisked was dark, possibly Italian or Greek. You'd have thought they suspected him of being Sacco or Vanzetti, sneaked down from New England.

I was glad they hadn't frisked us, and wondered what we'd do if they tried. It was obvious we were at their mercy, and for once my ignorance of our mission seemed a boon. All I knew was, there was little information they could beat out of me.

Corman pulled out his gold watch and made a show of checking the time. "I had expected a car, Kirk."

The deputy pointed to one coming down the street. The automobile turned in the lot next to the station and parked at the edge of the platform. A blubbery man in a brown fedora climbed from the front. As he moved toward the rear door, I saw that he, too, had a badge pinned to his dark coat. When the driver joined him, they opened the car door and seemed to finagle with something inside. Soon a small man emerged.

The man in the hat had handcuffed himself to the little guy. He gave a tug at the cuffs and they started walking toward the waiting train. The prisoner was wearing short leg irons, so it was hard for him to walk any way but herky-jerky.

"Who's Chaney got there?" Corman asked Kirk.

"He's taking the wop to the pen today."

"The wop?" asked Grant.

"Alberto Gatini. He murdered the prospector years ago."

"So, he's the one?" asked Corman.

"Yeah," answered Kirk. "He's another reason we're taking special precautions this morning. There's folks around that sides with the dago. They claim he's been framed. We don't want anyone trying to bust him free. Sheriff Chaney changed the whole schedule of taking him to prison. Most everyone believes the wop's going to Moundsville next week. He'll be gone before they know better."

"Sometimes Fred Chaney has brains," mumbled Corman, who kept his eyes on the sheriff and the prisoner as they drew nearer. Finally, he said, "Morning, Fred."

"Morning, Doc," said the sheriff with the cheery slur of a stump politician. "Mr. Briggs'll be happy you got here." Almost whispering, he added, "The old man's not well."

Corman ignored the medical report and asked, "So this is the prospector's murderer?"

"Yeah, and we're not taking no chances with the son of a bitch. I'm delivering him to the pen personal. He's a real fooler. Don't look like the kind to stick an axe in someone, does he? Got some folks convinced he didn't do it." Chaney took off his fedora and ran his fat fingers through his thinning blond hair. "Going to be another hot day. Got to be on our way. Train's waiting for us. I won't be back for a few days, Doc. After I unload the wop, I'm heading down to Charleston, to the capitol on some business. I've made Kirk here the chief deputy. If there's anything you need, just ask Josh."

Better for Josh Kirk to be chief deputy than Smithers, I decided as I glanced again at the two deputies.

Chaney pulled at the short handcuff chain and started walking toward the train. Gatini shuffled along, half a step behind the sheriff, like a slave being sold downriver.

A frail man in his fifties, it was hard to believe Alberto Gatini was roughneck dangerous. Maybe it was his colorlessness. If I'd been worried earlier about my general paleness, then the Italian had better stay away from mirrors. The pallidness of his olive skin must have come from sitting too long in jail. Still, he probably had more serious matters to worry about.

Chaney hauled Gatini up the steps and on board the Shawnee–Potomac train. The engine's whistle screamed, and soon the train left the station.

Over the steam engine noise, Kirk asked, "Are you ready to go to the hotel, Doctor?"

"You'll take care of my baggage, I assume," said Corman.

"Smithers'll bring it by later."

Corman took a step toward the car, then turned back. "Would you like to ride along, Professor?"

"Sure."

"Bring Professor Grant and Mr. Edmonson's baggage, too," Corman ordered Smithers.

Deputy Smithers' face boiled red, but even he was bright enough to keep his mouth shut. He knew he'd better not cross the big bossman's pal and physician any further.

Walking toward the black auto, I pondered the wisdom of all the professor/student crap on the train, of our cover as "folklorists." For the moment, it seemed Grant had known what he was doing. It certainly beat being frisked and grilled by Briggs' goons.

Corman took the front seat where the sheriff had sat. Grant and I were in the back, and as we rolled away from the station I imagined I could feel a sweaty dampness where Gatini had been sitting. We hadn't gone more than a block when Grant pointed out a building on our left. "I take it that's the sheriff's office and the jail."

Corman chuckled. "That's what it is, though Fred Chaney has to call it a 'branch office' with a 'holding tank.' Local politics, you understand. This isn't the county seat, and some of the old-timers are spreading the word that Chaney spends all his time here. They're trying to scare people into believing Blind Spring may be county seat one day and the courthouse will be moved here. Of course, that just might eventually happen. I assure you, Blind Spring is the whole ball of wax in this neck of the woods. There's no place else worth seeing."

The driver's muscles flexed as he steered a corner, and then we got our first real glimpse of the boomtown. Driving past storefronts, I felt a rawness in the air, or imagined I did. The place felt like Dodge City or some other cowtown from the dime novels I'd read as a kid, but the feeling wasn't one I could logically explain.

"What's the story on the Italian?" asked Grant.

Corman swiveled to face us. "You heard the gist of it. About five years ago, before Timothy and his son came here, a prospector named Lancelot Scott was murdered. They never caught his killer, and, ever since, there have been vicious rumors."

"Vicious rumors?"

"You must understand how these mountain people gossip. They distrust outsiders. They oppose progress. And, if the outsider happens to be wealthy like Timothy, it makes it all the worse. Some of them apparently believe Timothy had this prospector murdered so he could move in and take over. Nasty, foolish nonsense. But, how do you fight it? Timothy could have bought and sold the prospector ten times over. The point is, the rumors got to him and they bothered him. Timothy's a proud man. He didn't like the tarnish on his name. Last summer, he asked Chaney to reopen the old case, and the sheriff found the killer."

"Gatini?" I asked.

"Yes."

The driver seemed to be listening closely to our conversation, and I wondered if he'd report it back to someone. He turned another corner. Until then, we'd only seen the tent colony, the rickety houses, the clumsily built station, the sprawling corridor of storefronts, so I wasn't prepared for the new world that opened up.

The car pulled to the far side of the broad paved street and swung around in a U-turn, coming to a stop in front of the white porch that rose the full height of the Briggs Hotel. The tall brick building was certainly fine enough, as Corman had said it would be. It was obvious this was no rush job, no un-blueprinted shanty. In fact, the four-story structure would have made a substantial addition to any street in Washington, Baltimore, Richmond, or any of the other cities I'd seen.

"You can get out here," announced Corman. "I hope you'll enjoy your stay, and that you find this folklore you're after. I'll mention you to Timothy. He's a social creature in his own gruff way. He can be quite charming, with a whimsical sense of humor at times. But living in such a remote place, and being in poor health, can be hard on active minds like his."

"We hope to meet him," said Grant as he opened the car door. "We hope to meet him real soon," he mumbled to me as we walked up the hotel steps.

After the scene at the station, it was good to walk into a place as comfortably outfitted as the Briggs Hotel. Blind Spring might not turn out to be so bad after all, I told myself.

The black bellhop who led us into the elevator was about the first man I'd seen all morning who was smaller than me. In fact, he was so thin he made me feel like a weightlifter.

When the elevator doors opened on the third floor, he started down the hall so fast that Grant and I were immediately playing the tortoise to his hare. Grant, however, didn't care we'd lost our escort. We hadn't taken four steps before he halted, laughing. "Look at that door," he said.

I saw immediately what Dr. Corman had meant about his friend's sense of humor. Timothy Briggs, or someone, had shot a large wad of whimsy into the hotel's design. There were no numbers on any of the doors. Instead, on each was lettering in some sort of formal Old English script. Every transomed, dark wooden door was labeled with the name of a state. The first room we came to was *Nebraska,* which was followed in rapid succession by *Nevada* and *New Hampshire.*

The bellhop was waiting for us when we reached the end of the stretch. He'd already unlocked two rooms for us. Grant made some show of reading the rooms' names before looking at me and declaring, "You take *New Jersey*. I've been there too many times. I'll take *New Mexico*. I've never been there. Hell, it's only been a state for eleven years."

Even the bellhop cracked a smile as he handed us our keys and hurried back to the elevator.

Actually, *New Jersey* wasn't much different from *New Mexico*. Each sported a large bed and a private bath, something you weren't always lucky enough to find. The furniture was as brand new as the building. Briggs clearly wanted to impress his guests.

After we'd given the rooms the once-over, Grant and I went out on the balcony.

"We're lucky to have these rooms," he said. "If we were back the hall a ways, or in one of the interior rooms, we wouldn't have a porch to step out on. We can also get into each other's room without going through the hall."

"You think of all the angles," I said.

"You have to," he answered, moving to the side of the balcony and leaning over the white railing. "There it is."

"What?"

He pointed down into an alley that ran between the hotel and the next building. "The car we came in."

Sure enough, it was parked in the alley, right beside a side door.

"Knew there had to be a private entrance," said Grant. "You notice Corman didn't go through the lobby with us. He stayed in the car when it drove on. Besides, the public elevator only goes up to the third floor."

"I guess I didn't notice."

"You've got a hell of a lot to learn, Bill."

"I have worked out a thing or two."

"Yeah? What's that?"

"I figure we came to town to find out who killed this prospector years ago."

He didn't answer, so I took it a step farther. "You don't think this Italian, Gatini, did it."

Grant stared down at the car in the alley. "Our client doesn't believe Gatini did it. I don't know whether he did or not."

"Who's our client?" I asked, feeling as if I was finally on the right track.

"He wants to remain anonymous," said Grant, moving toward the balcony door of his room.

"Gatini didn't look like a murderer."

"What's a murderer look like? How many of them have you caught?" he asked, and then he shut his door behind him.

After a while, I went into *New Jersey* and laid across the bed. The mattress was firm, without the hills and gullies of other hotel mattresses I'd slept on. Tired from the travel of the last twenty-four hours, I could have fallen asleep right then, but I fought it off. Soon I was worrying about why it was taking so long for our trunks to be delivered from the station. Josh Kirk, Smithers, or some other deputy was getting plenty of time to rifle through our stuff. Not that it mattered. We'd been careful about what we'd packed. At least, we hadn't been frisked and questioned about why we were carrying guns. Still, I didn't like the notion of someone going through my underwear.

Finally, the knock came and my trunk was toted into the room by two bellhops. When they left, I glanced at the clock on the nightstand. We'd only been in Blind Spring an hour and a half.

I was still squatting by my trunk, checking its contents, when another knock broke the silence. I opened the door to find Grant. "You ready to tour this joint?" he asked. "It's always good to get a feel for the lay of the land."

We walked on up the hall, the long way around the third floor, past *New York, North Carolina, North Dakota, Ohio, Oklahoma,* and *Oregon*. Turning the corner at *Pennsylvania,* we kept going around the block, all the way to *Utah,* next to the elevator.

Grant pointed out that, unlike the elevator, the nearby staircase went up another floor, but the way up was cordoned off.

Grant stared at the steps for so long that I thought he was building up the nerve to leg over the rope and head on upstairs. Then a black maid came out of *Tennessee,* just down the hall. Over the pile of dirty bedclothes in her arms, she shot us an untrusting stare. Grant walked briskly to the elevator and pushed the button.

Down in the lobby, we settled into overstuffed chairs and he lit a cigarette. As he smoked, he watched the reflection of the desk clerk in the mirrors that lined one wall. The professor wasn't missing anything.

Two cigarettes later, he got up, and I followed him over to a hotel diagram on the back wall. Briggs was so proud of his airy staterooms that he'd framed a red, white, and blue floorplan. Forty-eight states in the old U. S. of A., forty-eight staterooms in the new Briggs Hotel. Twenty-four on the second floor, twenty-four on the third. I located *New Jersey* and *New Mexico,* then the rooms directly beneath us, *California* and *Colorado,* which were along a stretch that began with *Alabama, Arizona,* and *Arkansas.*

Grant laughed out loud again when he saw the label for the fourth floor. *District of Columbia.*

"Where else would the top man's mansion be?" he asked. "It's a shame there's no plan of the fourth floor for us to follow, Bill. I suppose that's to be expected. The President must be guarded at all times."

Then he looked over his shoulder at the desk clerk, who was busy stuffing mail into cubbyholes behind the counter. Coast clear, Grant bounded to his left, quickly opened a door marked PRIVATE, and pulled me into a closet-sized room. He was so animated, and I so tired and confused, that no one would have believed I was the younger man.

Inside, he silently pointed to a private elevator, then cracked open another door. After a long instant, he opened the door wider and we stepped out into the sun-splashed alley. The black car by the door was empty.

We walked up the alley and around the back of the hotel. A Negro in a white apron was peeling potatoes. I could smell food frying in the kitchen.

"This a good, safe place to eat?" Grant asked without skipping a beat.

The man grinned as we walked past him. He must have thought we were crazy. I couldn't have disproved him.

After circling the hotel, we reentered through the main door. If the desk clerk was worried about our reconnaissance, he didn't show it.

Grant led the way back down a hall and into a dining room, a large sparkling affair with silverware-laden tables and shining china with blue *B*s in the center of each plate. There seemed to be as many waiters as diners.

While we ate, I tried to get Grant talking by asking him about the coal mine wars that Deputy Josh Kirk and Dr. Corman had mentioned at the station. But Grant wasn't in the mood to deliver another history lesson. In fact, he'd turned serious, even gloomy. Where he'd been the bounding boy only minutes before, now he looked like he was shoving a lot of raw meat through a meat grinder and wasn't particularly happy with the sausage coming out.

All I could get out of him was, yes, there had been a "mine war," a series of mine wars, in fact. The bloodiest had occurred in 1921 when a United Mine Workers local had taken it upon itself to "liberate" the Logan County mines, Logan being the most anti-union county in the state—except, perhaps, for Murry, the county we were now in. Anyway, the miners had marched on Logan, and President Harding had sent in federal troops to put down the rebellion and retain order.

After leaving the dining room, we went back up to our

rooms. Grant deposited me at *New Jersey*'s door with directions that I catch up on my sleep and study the ballad book to perfect our cover.

Inside, I laid across the mattress again, and this time I couldn't keep awake.

I lost a good chunk of the day.

5

I awoke to the maze of ninety-degree angles where the *New Jersey* wallpaper met the *New Jersey* ceiling. Looking at it cock-eyed, it was easy to imagine the flower-covered walls flattened into the white ceiling, and the ceiling was the wall. If I rolled my head in the softness of the pillow, however, all would change and the walls would again be hotel walls, and the ceiling would again be a hotel ceiling, and there would be a thin border between the two, a dividing line, like a railroad track, and the tracks would converge in the corner, on a center.

What the hell was I doing in Blind Spring, West Virginia, tagging along behind Frank Grant?

I forced myself out of bed and, groggy from sleeping through a warm afternoon, went to the bathroom and filled the tub with water. Twenty minutes later, cleaner and more alert, I went out on the balcony for air.

When I leaned over the side railing, I noticed the Ford was gone from the alley. Nor did I spot it among those parked out front, though there seemed to be more cars than when we'd arrived. Some were dusty and splashed with dried yellow-brown mud, as if they'd been out in rough terrain. I remembered that Dr. Corman had said the railroad wizards were planning new tracks. Maybe they'd returned to the hotel after their day's work.

Wondering what Grant was doing, I walked next door to his room and knocked. When he didn't answer, I knew what I should have suspected all along: he'd slipped out on me. He'd been so eager to put me in my room, and then he'd gone out to work on the murder case alone, leaving me to sleep. Damn him.

With nothing else to do, I leaned against a white column and looked out on the town. My eyes landed on the powerlines that stretched down a hilly residential street and eventually hooked up to the hotel. Somewhere over the ridge was a power plant, another piece of the world that Timothy Briggs was creating . . . Coal mines, timbering, railroad expansions, an America-in-miniature hotel . . . . While the old man might be so ailing he needed his doctor close, he surely still had the drive for empire and money.

Alabama, Connecticut, Delaware, Iowa, Louisiana, Maryland, Virginia, Wyoming—all just rooms in one big house, and Briggs lived on top.

A car—the black one—came up the street and swerved into the alley. By the time I'd reached the side railing, it had come to a stop by the private entrance. The same husky deputy climbed out. From three floors up, he looked like an overdeveloped dwarf as he rushed around to open his passenger's door.

From any angle, the passenger looked like dynamite. Her legs emerged first. Like the singer in Union Station, she was wearing a short skirt. Pulled tight over her head was one of those fashionable close-to-the-skull hats, looking like a helmet and leaving only a fringe of her dark bobbed hair showing.

Just before she went in the side entrance, she tilted her head back and I could see the red of her lips and cheeks. Then, with an independent stride, she stepped inside and out of view.

I imagined her striding into Briggs' private elevator and being transported up, rising past the second floor, then the third, on up to the kingpin's suite on the fourth. Suddenly, Blind Spring felt better. It had its own good-lookers. Modern, up-to-date, 1920s women.

But who the hell was she? And why hadn't I met girls like her and the singer at the university? And what was the chance I'd meet her here?

I could have sworn I heard footsteps and voices, a door opening and closing up in the *District of Columbia*. Then, realizing the sounds were coming from the hall, I went back inside my room and edged the front door open a crack. Grant, his key in his hand as if he was about to unlock his room, was talking to the same bellhop who'd escorted us upstairs that morning. Before I could begin to follow their conversation, the bellhop was gone.

Grant stepped toward my door and shoved hard, nearly knocking me down. "You don't have to play eavesdropping games with me," he snarled, pushing into the room and slamming the door behind him.

"I wasn't eavesdropping," I said. "I heard something in the hall and took a look. Isn't that what I'm supposed to do?"

"You're not supposed to get caught at it," he said, leaning against a chest of drawers.

"I knocked on your door. You've been out and around while I napped. I should have been with you. Where'd you go?"

"Corman delivered."

"Delivered what?"

"The bellhop just gave me the message. We're invited upstairs for high tea with Briggs at four o'clock tomorrow. Corman must have talked us up nice."

"High tea?"

"Hell, don't be so literal. We'll get to see the White House tomorrow afternoon. That's a huge step." His long fingers tapped staccato against the chest. "Well, are we going to get some supper or what?"

"If you want. Seems like you're the one calling all the shots."

"At least you got that right," he said, rapping the chest sharply, like he was tired of waiting for me.

He turned and went out the door. I ran after him, past *New Hampshire, Nevada,* and *Nebraska* to the elevator.

6

We had beefsteak and fried potatoes in a small joint on the corner. Pushing back from the table, Grant said we were going for a walk. What he meant by a walk, however, wasn't a let's-get-some-night-air stroll. We might as well have been General Pershing's doughboys slogging across the Western Front. Except for one thing—Blind Spring lacked the storied charm of the wartime French villages I'd heard about. Blind Spring was too young and raw. Or I was.

We marched up the main street a while, backtracking ground we'd driven over in the morning. The street was called Briggs Boulevard. You build it, you name it, I guess. Every now and then we passed a building that was obviously old, though most of the structures clearly postdated Briggs. Still, there had been some kind of town before his coming, though it was getting harder to pick out.

Before we'd walked all the way to the station, Grant turned up a side street, and soon we were headed northwest, as best I could calculate. Eventually, we hiked down another street and seemed to be curving back to the main drag.

The whole time, Grant acted as if he knew where he was leading. We passed a gasoline station where the pumps advertised John D. Rockefeller's Standard Oil. Then he ducked down a path toward a huge barn. There was no doubt it predated Briggs. The faded sign over the door read: MCGRAW'S STABLE & BLACKSMITH SHOP.

Just inside the broad doorway was an anvil. We'd no more than gotten two steps beyond it when the stablekeeper piped up.

"You ain't wanting them horses tonight, are you?"

"Stay in your rocker, Ben," said Grant. "I don't expect we'll need them before tomorrow or Saturday."

Ben McGraw—the old man who Grant knew for some reason—stayed in his rocking chair. I doubted he'd have budged no matter what Grant said. He looked firmly rooted to the stable's dirt floor, his chair next to a potbellied stove. The weather was too warm for the stove to be fired up, but it was easy to picture him resting there in the January-February cold.

"You going up to see the widow again?" asked McGraw.

"Just may," answered Grant, uncomfortably glancing my way.

Who the hell was the widow?

"Ain't no crime to pay an afternoon call on Suze." McGraw laughed.

"She's a good source of mountain lore," said Grant, ever the professor.

"The best, for what you boys seem to be after. This the boy that'll be riding the other horse?"

"Yeah."

"He knows how to ride a horse proper, don't he?"

"He's an old hand."

"Not exactly," I said.

"Figured as much," said Ben McGraw. "These boys today, what'll come of 'em? They grow up with Henry Ford cars. But if you aim to go up in the mountains far, no car'll get you to some points, not with the roads—or lack of 'em—we got around here. This ain't the big city, as the slickers learn fast enough."

I guessed, to him, I was a slicker, though I'd grown up in a small town.

"I didn't say I can't ride," I said. "All I said was I'm not an old hand." Truth was, I'd done damn little horseback riding.

"Bill'll do fine," pledged Grant. "Look at some of the fools who've ridden horses far and wide."

"That's for sure," said McGraw. "Anyway, you ain't exactly going to be racing up those hills. Like I told you this afternoon, it's a long haul some places."

"I got that impression," said Grant. "Fellow on the train tried to scare us off. He warned us it's dangerous in the mountains, with the bootleggers and all."

McGraw rocked forward and spit a stream of tobacco juice on the dirt floor. Rubbing his hand across the gray stubble on his red cheek, he said, "That fellow could have told you right."

"It's that bad, is it?"

"Depends on who you meet and what you're looking for. Hell, they probably won't shoot you with no cause. You got your wits about you. Just be careful of the questions you ask."

"What are the wrong questions?" I asked.

"The questions people don't want to answer." He smiled. "The whiskey boys can get suspicious, it's true. Some's been making whiskey all their lives, and their daddies before 'em, all the way back to the Whiskey Rebellion. They always come down on the whiskey men, don't they? This Prohibition leaves a man colder than a witch's tit."

"I'm told we can find a whiskey man around town to buy from," said Grant.

"More than one of them."

"The widow mentioned one in particular."

"You'll find that one out near the company houses most nights." McGraw stopped talking and seemed to size us up a moment. Then he pulled a flask out of his pocket. "Want a nip?"

"Sure," said Grant, taking the flask and lifting it to his lips.

He swirled the liquor around in his mouth before he swallowed. "Not bad. I'll have to go find this guy and get my own."

"Best be careful, like I warned you," said McGraw. "He gets spooked easy by strangers. Briggs' men are always hot after him."

Whatever was in McGraw's flask had a stinging alcohol bite, not an aged whiskey fullness. I tried to swallow without expression, but my voice sounded weak, even to me, when I asked, "By Briggs' men, you mean the deputy sheriffs?"

"Silly to call 'em deputies." He spat out the words along with more brown juice. "Everyone knows a deputy sheriff is on the county payroll, and those boys ain't. They're mine guards, pure and simple. Ain't nothing but glorified mine guards with deputy badges tacked on their puffed-out chests. All them alleged deputies are paid by Briggs' money, and he don't want his miners getting drunk and turning rowdy any more than he wants 'em hearing union talk. Of course, it's alright for the hypocrite to have a full bar for medicinal purposes himself, and for entertaining. I'm sure Mr. Harding don't play Carrie Nation in private, neither."

"Must be bad times for Briggs," said Grant. "Moonshiners running amuck, and Sheriff Chaney thinks a union organizer's sneaked into town."

"So I hear. I suppose that's one more reason for the High Sheriff's thugs to be on the loose at all hours."

I handed the flask back to McGraw. "We met Chaney this morning. He said he'd be out of town a few days."

"There's the key, ain't it?" he asked, screwing the lid back on the flask and returning it to his pocket. "You think a West Virginia sheriff can afford to go traipsing around the country, going down to Charleston's best red-light establishments and all, if he ain't got other sources of income than a county paycheck?"

"He said he had business in the state capitol."

"Some favor for Briggs, probably. Then, at night, he'll curry his own favors. Fred Chaney never did amount to nothing worthwhile. He come back here after the war and saw Briggs was buying up the valley and dealt in with him, that's all. He got rewarded by being made sheriff. Briggs' money and the graveyard vote got him elected."

"He was taking a prisoner to the penitentiary this morning, an Italian," I said. "Alberto Gatini, wasn't it? Supposed to have killed a prospector years ago."

"So says Chaney and Briggs." McGraw stared at Grant. "You been up to the widow's. I reckon you know some think otherwise."

"Did you know this Gatini?" asked Grant.

"Yeah. He was alright. I had nothing against him. I'd say the old man just put pressure on Chaney so's he had to find someone to blame for the killing. Poor Alberto was who they picked. Look, I've lived here for sixty-four years. If you ask me, it's a goddamn shame they found coal. I liked this place better before it boomed. If they had to find coal, I'd rather Lancelot Scott was the one cashed in. I don't figure Alberto was no murderer. They just prosecuted him to the hilt. Regular county prosecutor wasn't good enough. Briggs paid for a special one. Then they made a big how-to of appointing a shyster for the Italian, though they said they was under no obligation to. They hired him one of them Fayette County models."

"What's that?"

"The kind that's like the lawyer who defended the same poor soul twice the same day. In the morning, he talked for the guy in a divorce case and lost when the wife claimed the fellow was impotent. In the afternoon, same lawyer, same client, lost a bastardy case in front of the same jury."

"You're saying Gatini didn't get the best defense?"

McGraw took out his flask again and had another sip. "I'm saying Alberto could have defended himself just as good, and he hardly knew any English."

"Then, who did kill Lancelot Scott?" I blurted out. On one side of my face, I could feel McGraw's eyes boring into me as hard as Deputy Smithers' had that morning. On the other side, I could feel Grant's spading in.

"That's the kind of query you don't go around asking when you hardly know a person, boy," said McGraw. "It could end you in six-foot-deep trouble. I thought the pair of you was out for old songs and stories."

"We are," said Grant, forcing a smile. "Five years back, before the Armistice, before Briggs came to town—that's an old story, ain't it?"

The stream of spit hit the earth. "Not old enough, maybe."

"So, tell us another," invited Grant. "You know an old song for our collection?"

McGraw cleared the tobacco from his mouth and took another sip of whiskey. He seemed to be searching his brain as he stuck the tobacco back in his mouth and the flask in his pocket. Before I knew it, he was singing in a creaky, aged voice that reminded me of my grandmother singing hymns.

"Real good, Ben," said Grant when he was through. "Never heard it before. You know more of it?"

"No, just heard a gandy dancer, a trackman, belting it one day. Jay Gould used to own railroads in West Virginia and western Maryland, you know."

"Can you sing it again so Bill can get the words down?"

I reached into my pocket, produced a small notebook and a pencil, and prepared to play stenographer like Grant and I had practiced. God, if you'd have seen me, you'd have believed we really were hunting folklore. The old man sang it again and it went like this:

Jay Gould's daughter said before she died,
"There's one more road I'd like to ride."
"Tell me, daughter, what would that be?"

"The Western Maryland to the Santa Fe,
The Western Maryland to the Santa Fe."

Jay Gould's daughter said before she died,
"Father, fix the blinds so the bums can't ride,
And if ride they must, let them ride the rods,
Let them put their fate in the hands of God,
Let them put their fate in the hands of God."

"Good song," said Grant, complimenting him again.

"I'd judge that's how the union organizer got in town," said McGraw.

"How's that?"

"He rode the rods, hopped off a freight."

"I guess Jay Gould didn't fix things good enough," said Grant.

McGraw laughed so hard that his mouth opened wide and the tobacco almost fell out, and I could see his brown-stained teeth.

"Ain't nobody can fix things that perfect," he said. "Not Jay Gould, not Fred Chaney, not Timothy Briggs, not nobody. Thank God, they can't."

7

We were walking away from the stable when Grant lit into me.

"You almost blew everything, Bill. You've got to learn to be careful. You've got to steer people the direction you want, not ask them point-blank questions. 'Who killed Lancelot Scott?' Jesus Christ! You saw McGraw's reaction. Now you see why I haven't told you any more than I've had to. The people we're working for want confidentiality."

"I'm sorry, *Professor,*" I said, a bit sarcastically perhaps.

"Cut the shit, Edmonson," he shot back in anger.

I tried to explain. "I just thought a direct approach might work."

"You're out in the world now, not in a state university lecture hall. You can get yourself killed. Hell, you can get *me* killed, and I wouldn't appreciate it."

I guess I almost hated Grant at that moment.

Without another word, we walked along one of those one-leg-long/one-leg-short streets where, due to the slope, the rooves on the left side never rose above the ground floors on the right. It was getting dark and, eventually, we came to a large well-lit building. The odor that hung around the place gave it away even if you happened to miss its BLIND SPRING BAKERY sign. Grant stopped, looked in a window, and the light bounced off his face so I could see he was still mad.

"You know I'm only trying to help," I said. "This is my case, too. I've done everything you asked me. So I asked a bum question? Fill me in. What'd this Suze, the prospector's widow, tell you this afternoon?"

"Lancelot Scott wasn't married," said Grant, starting to walk again.

"Who's the widow then?" I asked, catching up with him.

He was clammed up, and as we hiked, I could feel him glaring at me through the dark. I gave up trying to get him to talk, and he didn't say a word all the way to the company houses. By then, it was full night. There were no streetlights, as there were around the hotel. What should have been almost a full moon was made gloomy by a sheet of clouds, like the night before on the train.

The street of miners' homes was quiet at first sight, but as we stood and looked across the dirt road at the frame rowhouses layered up the hill, I could hear voices from inside. Windows were open to let in air and I saw the shadow of a man—no, maybe it was a woman—cross in front of a light. Then, just below us, a door opened and slammed. Soon a young man in a workman's cap was rushing by us, continuing up the hill until he was lost in the darkness.

"Follow the running man," whispered Grant.

We crossed the street and had only taken a couple of steps before the words were coming at us in pinpricks.

". . . Jesus . . . Railroad . . ."

The voice came from somewhere above us.

". . . wife . . . great . . ."

The man's voice grew louder, and the words began to come together.

"Lose . . . wife . . . think . . . great . . . Jesus Christ . . . great . . . lose . . . railroad. . . ."

I could hear the scuff of his limp before I could see him clearly.

"Evening, friend," Grant called out.

"Think you're great? Only Jesus Christ was great. Lose your railroad."

"Dammit, Harry, move it on!" yelled a man from one of the houses.

Harry staggered toward the closest window and bellowed, "Only Jesus Christ was great!"

Someone slammed the window shut.

Grant struck a match as if to light the cigarette in his mouth but held it at arm's length for a moment so we could get a glimpse of this Harry. I could barely make him out, but it looked like he had long white hair to his shoulders and, even on a June night, he was wearing a heavy wool coat. You could smell him from four feet away

"Lose your railroad, lose your wife, think you're great? Only Jesus Christ was great. You're deputies, are you? Always after me. Lose you railroad."

"We aren't deputies, Harry," said Grant, taking a puff of his cigarette as he dropped the match.

"Think you're great? Only Jesus Christ was great. How you know my name?" He pulled a quart jar out of his gray overcoat, unscrewed the canning lid, and took a big gulp.

"We just want a little whiskey ourselves," said Grant. "That's all we want right now. Where's the whiskey man, Harry?"

"Lose your wife. You can't have mine. Think you're great? Find your own. Only Jesus Christ was great. Lose your railroad."

"Take us to the man and I'll buy you another jar," said Grant.

"I ain't talking to you. Think you're great?" He began shuffling down the hill. "Only Jesus Christ was great . . . lose your railroad . . . lose . . . wife . . . great . . . Jesus . . ."

A burst of rowdy laughter came out a window and someone else yelled at the drunk to shut up.

". . . *railroad . . . wife . . .*"

Another form was moving toward us—the young man in the cap—with something under his arm—*a jar.*

"Say, we're looking for a little homebrew," Grant called.

"Look and ye shall find," answered the man, hurrying on.

Grant squinted at the corner ahead of us. I thought I could make out the outline of a man standing next to a horse.

"Let's do it," said Grant, dropping his cigarette butt and heading uphill.

The man's hand moved to his saddle as soon as he spotted us. He was preparing to ride away if he didn't like what he saw.

"Hey, don't run off!" Grant shouted. "We aren't cops or Treasury men."

"Cops and Treasury men never say they are," the man replied.

"Just want to make a small transaction, and to chat."

"I ain't no businessman, and I ain't looking for no transactions."

The whiskey man had a smoky hill-country voice that I bet disguised his toughness, but it couldn't disguise his suspicions. Everyone in Blind Spring seemed so damn suspicious of everyone else.

"Suze Chester mentioned you, and Ben McGraw said we could find you here," said Grant, squinting again through the dark at the guy. "I'm Professor Frank Grant, and this is my assistant. We arrived in town today."

"What are you professing?"

I wished I knew.

"Researching old songs and stories—the more complicated, the better. We aren't out to uncover stills, just tales, and if they happen to be in Italian, we'll translate. They don't have to be ancient lore. Five years is long enough ago."

"Sounds fascinating," said the whiskey man in a soft, flat voice. "So it's not brew you're after?"

"We could start with that. We hear you have top-grade stuff."

"Folks can be great misleaders. What's it worth to you?"

"I won't dicker. It's worth whatever you say it's worth."

The bootlegger opened the flap of his shirt pocket. Soon he was touching a match to the end of a hand-rolled cigarette. It was his turn to throw out a little light, and he held the match right up to Grant's face.

I couldn't guess what was going to happen. My grandfather had told me tales about moonshiners, how you rode up to a remote farmhouse where a cranky old lady was usually sitting on a porch with a shotgun across her lap, and how, if she let you pass, you headed up the road to a stump, collected your brew, left your cash, then highballed it home, never looking back.

Finally, the whiskey man tossed his match into the street and reached over to a basket slung over the back of his saddle. It looked like it was filled with straw, and he reached into it and produced a canning jar.

"This may ease your pain till something better comes along," he said, handing it over to Grant.

From down the hill came a whoop and a holler, followed by the sound of a slamming door, a loud blam, or was it a gunshot? We all turned our heads fast and saw what seemed to be a spotlight coming our way.

"Chaney's bastards," hissed the whiskey man as he jumped up on his horse.

Before I could blink, he was riding away amidst the sound of crashing jars. Grant grabbed my sleeve and pulled me over to the porch of the nearest company house. His left hand stuffed the whiskey jar in his pocket as his right reached inside his coat in a quick-draw motion he'd probably made a thousand times over the years. Then we squatted in the shadows of the porch. The door opened and a tall thin man peeked out.

"Cops coming," Grant whispered to him.

No questions asked, the guy waved us inside, where, the lights off and the door locked, we threw ourselves flat on the hardwood floor. Whether Grant had his pistol in hand, I couldn't see.

I heard a car stop out front. There were two voices, maybe three, but I couldn't make out what they were saying. The wall behind us was lit by a flash of light.

I imagined them out there, Deputies Kirk and Smithers, or a couple other goons from the station. I imagined them surveying the street, picking up a broken canning jar, shining a light on the whiskey pouring down the hill.

I waited for the knock on the door, not sure what was coming.

Car doors opened and closed again. A motor roared. Up the hill they drove.

I guessed they'd done their duty. They'd run off the whiskey man for the night. Briggs' miners were safe and, mostly sober, ready to turn in a productive Friday shift.

After a few minutes, our rescuer lit a lamp. He was older than me, but still under thirty. His short-cropped hair was so black that I couldn't tell if that was its natural color or if it was filled with coal dust. He was wearing coal-stained overalls and a blue workshirt.

He motioned for us to sit on mismatched chairs around the scratched-up table in the center of the room. The company house, new as it was, had the rough-and-ready bareness of a sharecropper's cabin I'd once been in.

"Everything okay, Kayce?" asked a young woman from the doorway to another room. She was younger than he was, plainly pretty, and had on a long dark skirt.

"Everything's alright, Polly . . . *I think,*" said the young man, this Kayce.

A baby cried in the other room, and Polly, her eyes still on Grant and me, closed the door.

Shoving aside a dinner bucket and a dirty cap with a miner's lantern attached to it, Kayce sat across from us. "You fellows new in town?"

"Got here this morning," said Grant. "Seems we keep running into the deputies, or mine guards, or whatever they are."

"If you stand out in the rain, you're bound to get wet."

"Does it always rain in Blind Spring?" asked Grant.

"Good bit of the time," said Kayce.

Grant made a show of looking around the pine-planked room His eyes landed on the dinner bucket. "So, you're a miner?"

Kayce nodded, but offered nothing.

"We saw a miner being carried off to the state pen this morning," said Grant. "Name was Gatini, I think. They were also on the lookout for United Mine Workers organizers. Sheriff Chaney apparently believes one's slipped into town. He seems pretty protective about who walks his gold-paved streets."

"Wouldn't know nothing about it," said Kayce real fast.

I felt a twinge of fresh anger at Grant. He'd just done to Kayce what he'd bawled me out for doing to McGraw.

"We should be thanking you for letting us come in out of the rain," I said, trying to fix things up.

"Just a roof over your heads temporary. Just lets you dry off before you go back out in the storm," said Kayce.

"Thanks, anyway," said Grant, reaching into his pocket and pulling out the jar of whiskey. He unscrewed the canning lid and offered the clear liquor around.

Kayce lifted the bootleg to his mouth. When he lowered the jar, he stared Grant level in the eye.

"Who'd you say you were?" he asked.

8

I was the one who eventually dragged Kayce's autobiography out of him, chunk by hard chunk. Me and the whiskey man's brew. Grant just sat quietly. Maybe he'd learned his own lesson about direct statements and questions.

His name was Kayce Powell, it turned out, and he was from Welsh stock originally, from coal mining people at Pompey Smash, the big mines west of the railroading city of Shawnee.

Just after the war, he and Polly had moved to western Pennsylvania, where he'd worked a stint in the steel mills. Then there'd been a couple hard years, so they'd moved on to Blind Spring on the promise of a job. He'd never intended to mine coal, or he wouldn't have left Pompey Smash in the first place, he said.

Kayce never progressed beyond relating the bare facts of his life. How he felt about mine guards, or Gatini, or the union organizer, he simply wouldn't say.

Later, walking back to the Briggs Hotel, I wanted Grant to remember how he'd backed the poor guy into a corner. After his earlier remarks to me, I wanted to rub it in.

"You could have gotten us killed," I said. "You almost lost

Kayce, scared him off. He never did completely drop his fear of us."

Grant walked faster, and so did I.

"Oh, I guess it didn't go so bad," I continued. "He was a nice guy. He saved us from the mine guards, and that's more than we could have hoped for. Glad you pulled out the whiskey. It loosened him up a notch. You should have asked him if he knew any old ballads."

"Why the hell didn't you?" mumbled Grant.

"You're the professor."

After a pause, he said, "Okay. I deserved that. But you did see more in his story than he told, didn't you?"

"What do you mean?"

"You must know what happened in the Pennsylvania steel mills after the war."

"Maybe I don't."

"Hundreds of thousands of steelworkers struck. U.S. Steel and the other companies wouldn't negotiate. They blacklisted anyone who didn't turn tail. Old Andrew Carnegie, the great philanthropist, had imbued the steel industry with the philosophy that you never deal with unions."

"You saying Kayce Powell was blacklisted and that's why he came here?"

"You can add. That would make him more nervous than usual about talk of an organizer in Blind Spring."

I was still mulling it over when we rounded the corner of the hotel. Lost in my thoughts, I didn't notice the deputy on the porch until he spoke.

"Evening, gents."

"Evening," replied Grant.

Like the other mine guards, this one seemed to have been hired solely for his heft. He rose from his seat and stepped toward us, his hand resting on the pistol in the holster strapped to his thigh.

"You boys guests here?"

"Yeah," said Grant. "We were out seeing the sights."

"The sights sparkle better in the daylight," said the deputy. "Never know what you'll come across roaming around late at night. This is still wild country."

"Thanks for the advice," said Grant, opening the lobby door.

Upstairs, Grant barely gave me a good night. "Study the ballads," he said before sliding into *New Mexico*.

Inside my room, I took off my suitcoat and caught my reflection in the mirror. The holster rigged over my shoulder looked strange and sinister. The job had at first seemed like a lark after years of classrooms, but at that moment it registered as something serious, dangerous. We'd bantered about it, but I knew Grant was right. *You could get killed.*

I took off the gun and laid it on the nightstand next to the red book. After slipping off my shoes, I padded over to my trunk and sifted through it again. Once more, I wondered if the deputies had searched it. Had they, in fact, searched our rooms while we'd been out? There was no way to know. I wasn't sure I even wanted to know.

I climbed onto the bed and propped myself up with the pillows. Determined to make Grant happy—and to read myself to sleep—I picked up the thick book. *English and Scottish Popular Ballads.*

How popular? Could you foxtrot to them? Certainly not like some modern-day hits, not like Paul Whiteman's Orchestra doing "Dardanella," not like the Original Dixieland Jazz Band tooting out a hot one-step. Probably not even as "popular" as the band we'd seen in Union Station.

I opened the lid.

Curly headed F. J. Child stared out at me. He appeared the perfect gentleman, aslant in his ornate chair, his seat of learning. *A ballad is a song that tells a story,* explained the introduction. Ballads, it was claimed, have no authors, but are composed by *the folk*—whoever they were. *The teller of the tale has no role in it,* it was written. *The story exists for its own sake.*

Six months earlier, I could never have predicted I'd be reading such stuff in a hotel room in a West Virginia boomtown, never would have guessed I'd be standing in a stable taking down a ballad about Jay Gould's daughter. Grant might harangue me about not being in a classroom any longer, but he was wrong. I was in his classroom. Studying books he'd assigned me. Listening to his lectures on the 1870s Erie Railroad wars and the Pennsylvania steel strikes. Dealing with his anger when I screwed up. I always had been a poor student, and never enjoyed sitting in lecture halls. That's why I'd quit. I guess I'd just wanted some adventure for once.

Professor Child's—*Professor Grant's*—book bounced on the mattress when I threw it down. I hopped off the bed and went out to the balcony.

Grant's curtains were closed and no lights burned inside. The streetlights glowing in the damp air confused my perspective, but it seemed like there were lights upstairs in the *District of Columbia.* Someone up there must keep late hours, I told myself.

Leaning over the railing, I could see the boots of the deputy stationed on the front porch. Tilting my head upward, I strained for some hint of voices above me. Were a man and a woman talking?

A car came up the street and pulled into the alley beside the hotel. A beefy man in a brown fedora climbed out of the passenger side and strutted toward the private entrance. If he spotted me staring down at him, he didn't show it.

I immediately walked over to Grant's balcony door and knocked. When he didn't answer, I knocked a little louder, figuring he wouldn't mind being awakened with the news that Sheriff Fred Chaney was back in town. For some reason,

Chaney hadn't gone to Charleston after ridding himself of his prisoner. For some reason, he'd doubled back to Blind Spring in the middle of the night.

But Grant didn't respond to my knocking, and the news was wasted for the moment. Either Grant wasn't about to be roused, or, goddamn him, he'd taken off again.

I was about to go out and try the hall door when something—an instinct, I don't know—made me glance into the alley again.

The deputy who'd driven Chaney back to town was opening a car door. A woman stepped from the private entry. She was wearing a long dark duster that almost reached her ankles. In the stodgy coat, in the odd light, she struck me as older than she had earlier that day. Yet I sensed she was the same woman. Perhaps she was simply tired.

She got in the car and soon it pulled around the back of the hotel. I waited for the vehicle to circle the building and pass in front of me, but it didn't. Apparently, it had headed off some other direction.

After a while, I went into the hallway and knocked at Grant's door. Still no answer. He definitely had slipped out on me. He sure had balls to leave the hotel right in front of the guard who'd tried to intimidate us. It occurred to me that he must have left as soon as I was inside my room or I'd have seen him stroll away.

Back in *New Jersey*, I stretched across the bed and wondered where the hell he'd gone. Back to the widow's for the night? Off on some other errand?

I tried to sleep but couldn't. The streetlights, the hall lights coming through the transom, the occasional headlights outside, caused streaks of brightness in the gray room. There was no way I could float off.

I turned the light back on and reached for the ballad book.

The thing opened to a page dog-eared by whoever had once owned it.

O where hae you been, Lord Randal, my son?

About as good a question as where was Frank Grant.

O I met wi my true-love, Mother, mak my bed soon, for I'm wearied wi huntin and fain wad lie down.

Whatever "fain" meant in long-lost ballad lingo.

And what did she give you, my handsome young man?

I stared at the words, the lines, the metered stanzas of what was probably the most famous of Child's popular ballads.

O I fear you are poisoned, Lord Randal, my son!

Smart mother.

For I'm sick at the heart and I fain wad lie down.

I flipped to another bent-down page.

O will ye go with me, my hinny and my heart? Will ye go with me, my dearie?

Then another.

O what hills are yon, yon pleasant hills, that the sun shines sweetly on?

I couldn't sleep, but I was so tired that the words, the songs, were all blending together.

O yon are the hills of heaven, he said, where you will never win.

I was lost someplace in a long-ago time, between night and day, running that line between ceiling and wall, half-asleep, half-awake.

O whaten a mountain is yon, she said, all so dreary wi frost and snow?

(O whare hae ye been?)

O yon is the mountain of hell, he cried, where you and I will go.

(My handsome young man.)

For I'm wearied wi huntin and fain wad lie down.

9

It was almost ten o'clock by the time I pounded on Grant's door the next morning, but the bastard still wouldn't answer. He'd either already gone out or he'd never returned.

Downstairs, the deskman informed me he hadn't seen the professor. And we had no messages.

I decided to play smart and take a page from Grant. So, I bought a Charleston paper from the stack on the counter and went out the door and down the street to the grille on the corner where Grant and I had eaten supper. I was the only one in the place that Friday A.M., and the short-order cook kept staring at me as he fried my eggs and bacon.

Ignoring him, I scanned the headlines, searching for coal-camp news. What there was of it came from towns and counties I'd never heard of. Mostly it concerned production figures—how many tons had been shipped out of which mine, by which railroad, on which day.

President Harding's cross-country jaunt got a big share of the front page. Harding had dubbed the trip "a Voyage of Understanding," and it was to take him all the way to Alaska. Maybe the Eskimos would understand him.

The President said he was out to make Americans grasp the

wisdom of his views about the morality of Prohibition, the World Court, and his oft-quoted "Return to Normalcy" following the war in Europe. If Grant was right, the President was also out to put some distance between himself and the steeping Teapot Dome, though the paper didn't breathe a word of scandal.

Apparently, Harding's ten-car train was stopping at every town so he could address the populace from the rear platform. His first speech had been in Martinsburg, West Virginia, only ten or twelve hours before Grant and I had railroaded through. From there, the presidential entourage had proceeded west to Shawnee.

I continued to read the paper from the state capital until I finally found what I was looking for: a short item buried at the bottom of page four.

MURDERER NOW AT PRISON

> Alberto Gatin, convicted murderer of prospector Lancelot Scott, was delivered to the penitentiary at Moundsville by Murry County Sheriff Fred Chaney on Thursday. Gatin's hanging is set for August. Governor E. F. Morgan is said to be considering a commutation of Gatin's sentence to life imprisonment.

Gatin. Hell, the idiots hadn't even bothered to get the Italian's name right.

I tossed the newspaper on the table, left the restaurant, and walked down Briggs Boulevard, wondering where the hell Frank Grant was and whether or not he knew the sheriff was back in town? Christ, I'd tried to tell him. If he didn't know, it wasn't my fault.

Blind Spring felt different to me than it had the morning before. The boomtown was no Dodge City. There were no gunfights in the streets—too many mine guards, I guessed—and no swinging-door saloons these Prohibition days. There weren't even many men on the street, though I passed a lot of women, mostly miner's wives with shopping baskets. Like Kayce Powell's wife, Polly, they were long skirted and modestly dressed.

It was easy to pick out which of the stores were company owned. At intervals along Briggs Boulevard were half a dozen large general stores with names like Briggs Emporium, Blind Spring Supply, Coal Camp Market. If there was any difference between them, I missed it. I wandered in and out of all of them, and they looked as interchangeable as factory-made parts.

In each, a long counter ran the length of a side wall. A few clerks milled around behind the counter, eying everyone who came through the door. Rows of shelves filled the bulk of the big rooms, stacked high with piles of workshirts, overalls, cheap boots, dinner buckets, lanterns, and rolls of fabric ready to be sewn into clothes. Elsewhere were canned goods, soaps, penny candy, bins of beans, and barrels of flour. In the back of each store, a butcher sweated over a chopping block.

The women carried their merchandise to the counters and watched as the salesclerks listed each item on a slender pad. Prices were higher than I was used to, and little cash changed hands. Once a purchase was duly recorded, the salespad was slid back into the appropriate family's slot on a metal filing contraption attached to the wall next to the cash register. Signs read BRIGGS COMPANY SCRIP ACCEPTED HERE.

Back outside, I walked along, paying little attention to the shopping bustle. Too little attention, it turned out. I scarcely noticed the group of kids tagging after me until I felt a tug at my coat sleeve and a young voice said, "Here, mister." He jammed a balled-up slip of paper in my hand, and I turned just in time to see them run away. There must have been seven or eight in the gang, all boys, some still in short pants, one carrying a baseball bat.

I uncrumpled the paper and stared down at the blockprinted message. A woman came out of the store nearby, and down the block, I thought I saw a badge flash. Closing my fist around the note, I crossed to the other side of the street where there were fewer people. Once there, I stopped in front of the movie theater and pretended to read the poster about the William S. Hart shoot-'em-up that was to play Saturday night. When all looked clear, I read the note again.

POMPEY SMASH TONIGHT.

Pompey Smash, the town Kayce Powell was from. No misunderstanding who wanted to see me. It was turning out to be quite a social Friday. Now I had two invitations. First, the "high tea" with Briggs at four o'clock, then the strange summons to the company houses later. A lot of help Grant was. Where in hell was he?

I was still cussing him when I saw her come out of a shop down the block. In her snappy short dress, it was obvious she was no miner's wife. Her clothes, her walk, her body, told me she was the woman I'd watched enter and leave the Briggs Hotel on Thursday.

I stuffed the note in my pocket and took out after her, but she was striding so fast that I lost her when she turned a corner. For a few minutes, I peeked in every shop window I came to. Then I went back to the place she'd come out of. It was one of the classier structures on the row and looked older than the slapdash bigger buildings. Mannequins in colorful new fashions stood inside the gleaming windows.

No customers were in the dress shop when I walked in. The tall middle-aged proprietress stared at me so hard that for a moment I felt like Charlie Chaplin's tramp.

"May I help you?" she asked in a deep, accentless voice.

I tried not to be any more intimidated by her than Grant had been by the cop on the hotel porch. "The young lady who just left . . ."

"Yes?"

"She dropped something on the street. I'd like to return it to her. You don't know her name and address, do you?"

"If you'll leave it with me, I'll see that she gets whatever it is."

"I'd prefer to return it myself," I said, patting my coat pocket gently, as if it contained something valuable. "I'm sure she'll want it back."

"Are you new in town?" asked the shopkeeper, never taking her eyes off me.

"I arrived yesterday on business."

"Where are you staying?"

"The Briggs."

On business at the Briggs Hotel must have been the right answer, for she finally said, "I imagine it's alright to provide you with Miss Bascomb's address." She wrote *Miss Bascomb, 117 Dutters Drive* on the back of a sales slip and slid it across the counter. "If you would like a gift for your lady friend," she said, "we have the best selection of clothing and lingerie in Blind Spring. We can order anything we don't stock."

"I'll remember," I said as I went out the door. Once outside, I felt like I'd won a small victory, but I didn't know why. Hell, I didn't even know why I'd gone through the charade of getting the young woman's name in the first place.

Miss Bascomb. So, she wasn't a Briggs. Not a wife, not a daughter. Where *did* she fit in? And, other than my own curiosity, did she matter at all?

The sun should have stood midday high by then, but instead there was a murkiness to the air as I headed back to the hotel. It wasn't raining, but the clouds had returned to stand guard. I couldn't tell if it would storm or blow over.

In the lobby, the desk clerk again said he'd seen no sign of

Professor Grant, and we still had no messages. Upstairs, I got luckier.

A maid was coming out of my room and going into Grant's, the same black maid who'd watched us suspiciously the morning before. She left the door ajar, so I just pushed it open and stepped in like it was my room. If she knew better, she didn't show it. In fact, she didn't even blink when she came out of the bathroom, a towel in her hand, and saw me.

"Your bed don't need made. Don't look like you slept in it."

"It's fine," I agreed. "Maybe you can help me. I'm supposed to see Mr. Briggs this afternoon. Where would I find him?"

"Why, you just go up the stairs, that's all. You won't have no trouble finding him."

"Nice town, Blind Spring," I said, fishing for some reaction.

"Some likes it," she answered as she closed the door behind her.

10

The nearer it got to four o'clock, the more I hated Grant. When there were only ten minutes left, I accepted my fate. I'd have to face Timothy Briggs on my own.

I guess I could have flagged down a bellhop and sent a message upstairs canceling the tea party, but it didn't seem like the smartest thing to do. I wasn't sure when I'd get another chance to meet the big man.

As I'd waited in Grant's room, I'd ransacked his trunk and chest of drawers, looking for something unusual, anything, to give me more hints about what we were supposed to be doing. But there was nothing, not even a ballad book to hoax anyone into believing we were folklore scholars.

For a while, I'd sprawled across the bed, and I hadn't even bothered to smooth out the mussed-up spread when I stood up. Let the son of a bitch worry about who'd been sleeping there.

At five to four, I went out the door, telling myself that, once high tea was over, I'd visit Ben McGraw and try to coax the widow's address out of him, just as I'd gotten Miss Bascomb's. If I had to, I could spend a bundle of time at the stable easing the info out before trekking on to Kayce Powell's.

At the roped-off staircase, I climbed over the cord and

headed up. A deputy sheriff was sitting in a chair facing the stairwell and the private elevator. He studied me without saying a word.

"William Edmonson," I announced. "Mr. Briggs is expecting me."

"Wasn't there supposed to be two of you?"

"Professor Grant is unable to come."

The mine guard slowly stood up and led me down the hall. His heavy-heeled boots thudded against the carpet with each step.

The layout of the fourth floor was pretty much like that of the second and third, except the rooms weren't marked in any way. We rounded a corner, passing the rooms that would have been Grant's and mine downstairs, and then we hiked up the long front hallway. The doors of the interior rooms—what would have been *Virginia* through *Wyoming* on the third floor—were open. At one point, I peeked in at a library filled with leatherbound books. I'd never seen a place quite like it before. But, then, not many residences took up the top floor of a hotel.

At the end of the hall, the deputy knocked on a door.

"Young Mr. Edmonson, come in," said Dr. Anders Corman, swinging the door open, then closing it behind me.

The dimly lit room wasn't at all what I'd expected. It wasn't the slightest bit fancy, and what light there was came from a shaded lamp on a desk along one wall, or flowed in through the open balcony door.

Corman motioned for me to sit on a leather chair. "Timothy," he announced, "this is William Edmonson."

I didn't see who he was speaking to until a grunt came from the bed near the window. The old man was so thin you could have sat on the covers without feeling a bump. The only proof of his being were his head and shoulders resting on a pile of pillows. The head was so enormous that it was hard to imagine it being attached to anything, let alone the frail body under those covers.

"Where's the other one?" demanded Timothy Briggs. There was certainly nothing frail about his voice.

Corman turned to me. "Where *is* Professor Grant?"

"He sends his regrets. He couldn't come."

"I hope he's not ill," said Corman. "I could drop down and see him, perhaps give him some medication if he needs it."

"Big medicine man," gruffed Briggs. "Never far from his black bag."

"Grant'll be fine," I said without further explanation.

Through the balcony door came a man with a drink in his hand. He was in his late twenties and as impeccably dressed as Dr. Corman, causing me to remember I was still wearing the clothes I'd trooped around town in.

"This is Jim Briggs," said Corman. "Actually, he's Timothy James Briggs, *Junior*."

"Nice to meet you," I said, but there was no reply.

Tall, solid, with slicked-down brown hair, Briggs Junior had a moping expression that made it clear he didn't want to be there. Looking at him, and then looking over at the old man, I no longer had any doubts about who Miss Bascomb had been visiting in the *District of Columbia*.

Jim Briggs must have felt my eyes on him. He dropped into the chair by the desk and asked, "What is it you're doing again?"

"Professor Grant and I are folklorists," I said. I fed him the line that Grant had fed Corman on the train. If the doctor minded the repetition, he was too much the gentleman to show it. "Murry County's a gold mine for researchers like us," I concluded.

"I'm glad to hear it's a gold mine for something," said young Briggs.

"Hell, stop complaining!" growled the old man. Then the head—it really was enormous—revolved toward me. "My son is spoiled, Edmonson. He doesn't like coal dust on his shoes, though he loves the money it brings in. He'd rather be back in Philadelphia with his late mother's family, attending socialite balls. Ignore his griping. Tell me more about this notion of yours."

"It's just that the farther you go into the mountains, the more you find people clinging to old traditions. The remoteness creates isolated pockets, and isolated pockets preserve the old ways."

"The remoteness causes senility, too," said Briggs Junior.

"Shut up," grunted his father. His eyes fixed on Corman. "Get me a cigar."

"I've told you not to smoke," said Corman.

"You *asked* me not to smoke," corrected Briggs. "Goddamn it! Get me a cigar!"

Both Briggs Junior and the doctor knew not to push the old man too far. The son opened a box on the desk, lifted out a cigar, and handed it over to Corman. Then there was a long rigamarole of getting it in Timothy Briggs' mouth and lit.

As I watched, I found myself admiring the old man for some reason. No son was going to complain to his face about living in the empire he'd created. No doctor was going to tell him what he could or couldn't do. At the same time, I realized those same qualities could make him a mean bastard to the people under his thumb.

"Go on," Briggs said to me between puffs on his cigar. He had the rough voice of a man used to making direct statements, not mouthing social niceties.

"Well, a lot of the old mountain families trace back to the Scotch-Irish and English frontiersmen from before the Revolution," I began. It was time to milk our cover. "Some believe there's a Celtic flair to their traditions. Researchers have found they sing some of the same ballads that Professor Child collected in Britain." I wished at that moment that I'd brought the ballad book to wave. "Of course, the songs change over generations and distance, but they change in Britain, too. For instance, there's a song usually called 'Gypsy Davey' in the New World. It's about a minstrel who lures away the lord's daughter. In English versions, it's unclear if they get away, which says something about their view of the world. Sometimes, the girl has second thoughts about the luxury she's abandoned. But, in America, the gypsy and the girl almost always escape, which says something about our view of the world."

"Makes me glad I don't have a daughter," said Briggs.

"How boring," said Briggs Junior.

"You're boring," the old man replied. Then he inched up higher on his pillows, removed the cigar from his mouth, and it was my turn to be cut off at the knees. "So why are you out to preserve these backward old ways?"

"Because . . . because the Ford cars and movie theaters and radios and Victrolas and all the rest are changing the world. The modern world is taking over."

"Good for it," mumbled Jim Briggs.

"I say good for it, too," said the old man. "But I can tell you've got a brain, boy, which is more than most young men I meet. If you ever decide to do worthwhile work, come see me."

A knock at the door saved me from having to answer. Dr. Corman stepped out into the hall to talk to someone and, a moment later, returned with a ledger in his hand.

"The bank's sent its weekly report," he said to Briggs.

The head nodded toward the desk, and Corman dropped the ledger on top of a stack of papers. Then he went over to a table loaded with refreshments. "Coffee or tea?"

"Something with a bite," demanded Briggs.

"A little sherry, perhaps," Corman told him in a tone more cautious than it had been about the cigar. "Don't overdo it, Timothy."

The head didn't answer and, when Corman looked at me, I said, "Sherry's fine."

"Whiskey," muttered Jim Briggs, handing his empty glass to the doctor.

Corman poured three glasses of sherry from a crystal decanter. Then he sorted through the bottles on the table until he found the right one and poured Junior a glass of whiskey. Playing host, he distributed the drinks and butlered around a tray of sweets and little sandwiches that had been sitting next to the coffee urn.

I hadn't eaten since breakfast, so I wasn't shy about grabbing up some of the goodies. It wasn't until I'd already taken a bite that I realized I was the only one eating. The old man and Corman seemed content to sip at their sherries. The son had downed his whiskey in three gulps and was on his way over to get a refill. Ben McGraw was right. There was no Prohibition in the Briggs Hotel.

"Have you had any luck yet finding this lore?" Corman asked.

"A stableman sang us a song last night."

"McGraw?" asked Briggs Senior.

I nodded.

"Old songs are about all the bastard's good for," the old man grumbled. "He's one of the biggest troublemakers in town, at least until recently. I once offered him an arm and a leg for a farm he owns south of town, but he refused to sell. Gave me a cock-and-bull story about how long it had been in his family. Jesus Christ, it's just a tumbled-in log cabin and some fallen-down fences. There's the old ways for you."

"We didn't spend long with him," I said. "We were arranging for horses for when we go up into the hills."

"I warned them about the moonshiners and their stills," said Corman. "They didn't seem to take me seriously."

"I wouldn't go tramping around in the hills for a million dollars," said Jim Briggs.

"That's why you'll inherit money instead of earning it," snapped his father.

Old Briggs' hand trembled a little when he raised the glass of sherry to his lips and sipped. Then he looked at me again. His eyes were as commanding as his voice. "Doctor's correct. The stillers are outlaws. Fred Chaney's got his hands full dealing with them. They don't seem to understand Prohibition's the law of the land."

"We met Sheriff Chaney and some of his deputies at the station yesterday," I said.

"I've heard, and I won't apologize for the trouble they put you through. It was necessary. We believe there's a communist organizer in town. You and this Grant didn't pick the best time to visit, Edmonson. I half expect the James Gang to start holding up trains."

"He was taking a prisoner to the state penitentiary. It was in this morning's paper."

"Yes, the Italian. Sad affair, from before my time. Fred Chaney does a creditable job." A smile opened on the big head. "I have a bit of lore for your collection, boy. You know what a blind spring is?"

"No."

"You're in Blind Spring and you don't know what a blind spring is? How about that? Well, for your information, a blind spring is an underground stream that miners come across when they're tunneling. It seems that, decades ago, when the first man tried to mine coal here, he hit a blind spring and gave up. They just marked all the old maps 'Blind Spring.' Until I came along, no one had given it much of another try."

What about the prospector, Lancelot Scott? I asked myself. If the rumors about him being removed for Briggs' benefit were true, then he must have been trying.

Briggs turned suddenly to Corman. "Where's that nigger?"

The doctor went out into the hall again and returned after a few minutes with the same bellhop I'd seen talking to Grant on Thursday afternoon. Except now he was carrying a cheap scratched-up guitar.

"We have a treat for you, folklorist," said Briggs. "Simpson here has a song, a better one than you got from McGraw, I'm sure. Move, Jim. Let the boy sit down so he can play."

"Shit," said Briggs Junior as he surrendered his seat to the bellhop.

"Now, sing the man the song," ordered Timothy Briggs.

Simpson positioned himself in the chair and silently fingered his guitar, getting ready. From my angle, he appeared a hunched, narrow form, silhouetted somewhat by the open balcony door. In the weak light, it was hard to read the expression on his face, but I thought he seemed almost as gloomy as Junior.

He wasn't a great guitarist, or, if he was, he was uninspired that Friday afternoon. Mostly he strummed a few chords, what sounded to my ear like a simple blues. Not that it mattered, really, because the words were the whole ballgame, and I rapidly grasped why Briggs had called Simpson in. There was the old man's sense of humor again.

The bellhop sang about riding a train into Mister Briggs' wonderful, thriving town. Everything was heaven. Jobs galore. Fine folks walking the fine streets. Busy well-supplied stores offering plentiful credit. A grand hotel. Booming mines. And, always, the chugging Shawnee–Potomac trains.

I recalled my first impressions of Blind Spring. How I'd felt about the deputies at the depot. How they'd later chased the whiskey man. How Grant and I had fled into the safety of Kayce's house, out of the rain for a time. How the maid had said, "Some likes it."

I hoped Simpson would get a bonus as big as the old man's head for his song.

Throughout the entire performance, a satisfied grin was slashed across that big head, making it look like nothing so much as a saw-toothed pumpkin. When it was over, the old man ordered, "Sing it again, boy," and, so, Simpson did.

As he sang his encore, my eyes went to the large map hanging on the wall above the huge flat-topped desk. On the map, Blind Spring's mining, prospecting, and timbering areas were clearly marked in different colors—a rainbow of enterprise.

Another knock hit the door.

This time when Corman stepped back into the room his face seemed white. Simpson stopped singing. Even Briggs Junior perked up.

"Sheriff Chaney wants to see you," Corman said to me. "Deputy Smithers is out in the hall waiting to drive you to the office."

I felt like Gypsy Davey called before His Lordship, or Robin Hood being hauled before the Sheriff of Nottingham.

11

Fred Chaney was leaning back on two legs of his chair, his feet propped up on his desk. The balancing routine had to be something he practiced. Still, the sheriff was oddly out of shape for a cop in his early thirties. It was obvious he let Deputies Kirk, Smithers, and the others do all the real work. If his beer belly had swayed to one side, he'd have been thrown out of kilter and would have rolled off the chair and onto the floor, maybe to bust open like an oozy soft-boiled egg.

The sheriff's office might have been just a "branch" office, as Corman had told us, but it looked like a police office to me. I was sure the "holding tank" beyond the heavy metal door looked, for all the world, like a jail.

Chaney's liquidy blue eyes locked on me as I took a seat in front of him. Leaning against a wall on either side of me were Deputies Kirk and Smithers.

"You William Edmonson?" asked Chaney.

"Yeah."

"We got bad news."

"Yeah?"

Later, I'd feel dumb because I'd had no inkling.

"Frank Grant is dead."

"Christ."

I don't know how much time went by without anyone saying anything. Even through my daze, I could sense the cops' eyes on me.

"I suppose you don't know nothing about it?" Chaney finally asked in a flat, calm voice.

I shook my head no.

"When was the last time you saw the victim?" asked Chaney.

"Victim? Was Grant murdered?" I managed to ask back.

Chaney's blond head nodded. "Maybe. We're trying to sort it out. When did you last see him?"

"Last night. Close to midnight, one way or another. We'd come back from a walk and gone up to our hotel rooms."

"Deputy Jenkins was on the hotel porch. He confirms he saw them," Kirk told Chaney.

"Where'd you walk?" Chaney asked me.

"All over," I said, not wanting to fall into a trap, not wanting to mention the whiskey man and Kayce Powell.

"Come on, open up. It could be important. We *are* the police, you know."

"We went down the main drag, then over to the stable to line up horses, then just wandered around town."

"McGraw's stable?"

"Yeah."

"You didn't run into no one, did you? Didn't get in an argument or nothing?"

"No, nothing really happened," I answered, again avoiding any mention of our trip to the company houses. "Just a walk. Look, you haven't told me anything. How did Professor Grant die? Where'd you find his body?"

Chaney slid his feet off the desk. His boots hit the hardwood floor with a whack and his chair settled on all four legs. Leaning forward, his pudgy arms on the desk, he said, "We weren't the ones found him."

"Who did?"

"The story could be longer than a whore's dream, so I'll cut it brief. All we know for sure's the body was discovered this morning in a coal car in Wild Stream, a few counties north of here."

"In a coal car?"

"Yeah. Buried in the coal. They say the body was mangled pretty bad. No way anyone could have recognized your friend, this professor. They found a wallet in his pocket, so they learned his name was Frank Grant. They wired all around the state, and Josh Kirk here remembered you boys arriving yesterday."

Chaney swiveled around to a small table behind him. He pushed aside the fedora on it and picked something up. Turning back, he handed me a wallet. "They sent this down on the last train. You might as well have it."

I opened the scarred leather billfold. Grant's money was still inside. He'd been careful to split up our expense money before leaving, saying it was safer that way. A man could get robbed and killed if he showed too much cash, he'd said. But whoever had killed him hadn't killed him for his bucks.

"He walked around with a lot of funds," said Chaney.

"We needed travel money. We were planning to spend most of the summer here."

"Didn't have much identification, only a little name card."

"I guess the professor didn't carry around his diploma with him. Look, how'd he end up in the coal car?"

"That's the mystery, ain't it? Seems the train left Blind Spring about six this morning. It had loaded up at the East Works during the night. They left off a couple cars in Wild Stream and, a few hours later, some guy spotted a hand sticking out through the coal."

I must have flinched, because Chaney stopped talking for a minute. When he started again, his voice was softer. "You know, it was just chance he was in one of the cars left at Wild

Stream. The body could have gone on to Pittsburgh or New York and been dumped in a furnace or something, and we'd never know what happened to him. Why didn't you report him as missing?"

I stuttered around some. "I . . . I just figured . . . figured he was off on his own somewhere. It's been less than a day."

"Didn't you think it was strange he didn't go up to see Mr. Briggs with you?"

I shrugged. "Any idea how he was killed?"

"Crushed by the coal. Couldn't you figure that? They're doing an autopsy up in Wild Stream, but the first doctor who saw the body didn't find no bullet holes or nothing."

Judging from the way Chaney looked at me, I must have flinched again.

The office door opened and two more mine guards came in, carrying a trunk—*Grant's trunk.*

"This is all the stuff from the hotel room, Sheriff," one of them said.

"Take it in the munitions room," Chaney told them. Then, to me, he said, "We figured we'd look through Grant's things for evidence. Besides, I didn't think you'd want to pay for an empty hotel room. We've checked him out."

Smithers opened a door and the two deputies edged the trunk through the doorframe. As soon as they had left, Chaney pushed himself to his feet and went into the other room. I followed.

The room was a regular arsenal. Gunracks lined the walls and entire corners were filled with stacked boxes of ammo. Chaney and Briggs were running a full-scale army, a fact I realized I should have already known.

Smithers opened the trunk and began going through its contents as Chaney and Kirk watched. "Just clothes," he said after a minute, dropping the lid on the trunk. He sounded mad that he hadn't found anything.

"I'll ask you right out," said Chaney. "You know any reason why this professor disappeared, or have any idea who might have bumped him off?"

"No."

"Did you ever work for a labor union?" asked Chief Deputy Kirk, jumping into the act.

"No. We told you the truth at the station. We came here to collect folklore."

"How about Grant? Did he ever work for a union?" asked Chaney.

"Not that I know of," I said, which, for once, was the whole truth. "I don't know why you're so convinced we have something to do with a union."

"I'm charged with enforcing the law in this county," said Chaney. "You haven't lived through the things that have happened in West Virginia since the war. Two years ago, a whole army of union miners marched on Logan County. They come out of the hollows with their daddies' old muskets in their hands and commandeered trains and killed some Logan deputies. Nothing like that's going to happen in Blind Spring as long as I'm around."

"We had nothing to do with anything like that."

"You better not," said Kirk.

"If I was you, boy, I'd be thinking of leaving town," said Chaney. "We couldn't protect Professor Grant, and I don't know we can protect you. Too many strangers just muddy the waters. There's too many outlaws around—bootleggers and union organizers and you name it. Could be some anarchists who wanted to save the wop. That's why I took him to Moundsville ahead of time."

"I figure I'll be staying in Blind Spring a while longer," I said. "I'll at least be staying until I find out what happened to Grant. I may even continue our research, since I'm already here."

"Just remember I warned you," said Chaney. "You seem alright. I don't want nothing to happen to you. You should have a long life ahead of you."

"What do I do about Grant's body and his stuff?" I asked.

"I guess you can have the body after the autopsy, if you want to make arrangements with the Wild Stream authorities. We'll keep the trunk here till you tell us where to ship it."

"Is the telegraph office over by the station?" I asked.

"Yeah. Deputy Kirk can show you the way."

"I'll find it," I said, brushing past Kirk as I went through the door.

12

GRANT IS DEAD.

My hand was shaking as I wrote the note, and the telegraph operator must have known there was something wrong. I labored over the words so hard that he probably thought I was illiterate, but it was a struggle just to get a few phrases together.

GRANT IS DEAD. BODY IN WILD STREAM, W. VA. PLEASE ADVISE.

The telegraphman didn't blink as he tapped out his dots and dashes. It was as if he didn't realize the message was an SOS. I didn't fully trust him. He could've easily reported everything I wrote, or said, straight back to Chaney. All of Grant's lessons were tumbling in on me.

The address I'd given was untraceable, according to Grant. I guess he'd played detective too often, alone in too many towns where the deck was stacked and the sheriff had an armory. When he'd made me memorize the "safe house" address, he'd told me it had been his idea. There had to be a place to wire, a place that on the surface had nothing to do with the detective agency.

When the telegraph operator was done tapping, I paid him. I got a fresh chill when I reached into my pocket and felt Grant's battered wallet. Then I went out the door and sat on a bench facing the railroad tracks. I sat there quite a while, trying to get my bearings.

Dead.

I could see both the station platform and, a block up the street, the sheriff's office. Deputy Smithers was loitering outside the office. I could've sworn he was watching me.

Slowly, other mine guards began showing up. They stood around with Smithers, and when there were about a dozen of them, they began walking toward the depot, toward me.

At that moment, I heard the low roar of a distant engine. The nearer it got, the louder the noise, as the rumble bounced off the hills on either side of Blind Spring valley.

The deputies drew closer, and so did the train. I could see the smoke from the engine's stack, and then the Shawnee–Potomac engine itself, slowing, brakes squealing.

The deputies passed me and lined up along the platform. Smithers hung back under the eaves of the station not far from me, silent.

The train halted in a hiss of steam. A handful of people, mostly men, began stepping down from the passenger cars. Deputies walked up to each of them. "Name?"

"None of your business," said a dapper little guy in his fifties. He was smaller than me, no more than five-five and a hundred and twenty pounds, a salesman maybe.

Smithers rushed over to him. "Don't give us no trouble. If you got nothing to hide, you got nothing to fear."

"What's your name, Deputy?" challenged the guy. "I'll report you to your superiors."

Sure.

Smithers' hand closed around the fellow's upper arm and just about raised him off the platform. "Your name, boy?"

"Go to hell."

The little guy had guts, you had to give him that.

Smithers muttered something under his breath, and the man said something back, and Smithers pushed him backward until he stumbled off the platform and ended up in the ballast along the tracks.

I stood up and started toward them, but another mine guard moved in front of me. "Stay out of it."

The man hauled himself up out of the ballast and, limping, climbed back on the train. When he got back to his office, wherever it was, he'd have a horror story to tell.

Just as I would.

The train chugged out of the station, just like in Simpson the bellhop's song. The deputies began to disperse. A car came and picked up three passengers who'd survived the gauntlet. To take them, I guessed, to the Briggs Hotel. Smithers stalked around the platform for a few minutes, then headed back toward the sheriff's office.

Hell of a town I was in. Like the ballad in the book said: *Yon is the mountain of hell.*

I got up from the bench. I couldn't just sit there with my head full of blues. I knew I had to get going. There were things to do. I'd talk to Ben McGraw, then go to see Kayce Powell and learn what was on his mind.

I guess I was halfway to the stable when it hit me I was being followed. Grant would probably have noticed the noiseless shadow in a quarter of the time. Still, I knew who it was. *Smithers.* The one with the yellow eyes. The one who talked dumb and pushed people under train wheels.

He was careful to give me a block's rein, but he stuck with me. No matter what I did, I couldn't shake the son of a bitch. If I stopped, he stopped. If I turned a corner, he turned a corner. Once I even doubled back to let him know I'd spotted him, but Smithers too doubled back to let me know he didn't care. He probably *didn't* care. After all, I was the one in trouble, not him.

I had no idea how I'd lose him before I went to the company

houses, but all my maneuvers were just eating up time. Finally, I gave up on the dodge and went straight to the stable. There was nothing odd about arranging for a horse.

Ben McGraw wasn't in his rocking chair. When I heard sounds from the back of the place, I followed them. He was stooped over, cleaning out a stall, and stood up when he saw me.

"Sorry about Grant," he said.

"So you've heard."

"Whole town's probably heard by now."

"There's a deputy tailing me."

"Just one? You mustn't be more than a splinter in their finger."

He ambled toward the front door and leaned on his anvil, pretending to fiddle with a chaw of tobacco. Eventually he wandered back in my direction.

"One of Briggs' bullies is out there alright," he said.

"Smithers."

"So that one's Smithers. He ain't been around long, but I heard of him."

"What'd you hear?"

"He used to be a blackleg, according to the story."

"A blackleg?"

"A state cop. They wear black leggings. The governor started a state police force after the war. Hired a bunch of veterans. They come into their own during the mine wars. They and the feds was about the only law around. Story is, this Smithers got mustered out for beating up too many folks. He was too much of a maverick for the state to keep on the payroll."

"Believable," I said. "What do I do about him?"

"You could shoot him. Why the hell you asking me? I'm just an old man. Why don't you go back to the hotel and go to bed?"

"I can't . . . I've . . . I've got an appointment to keep."

"Where's that?"

For some reason I can't explain, I told him. "Got to go over by the company houses tonight."

"You ain't no lore hunter, are you? I knew from the questions you was asking. College professors don't get themselves killed."

I didn't answer. Feeling like I'd made another mistake with him, I started for the stable door. My plan was to lead Smithers back to the hotel, then find some way out again.

"There's a back way to the company houses," said McGraw. "You can take a horse if it'd do you any good."

"Not tonight." I didn't want to worry about parking a horse near Kayce Powell's house. "I'll need that horse tomorrow. And directions to the widow's. Tonight, I'm on foot."

McGraw tilted his thumb toward the rear door. "You go out that way. Top of the rise, there's a narrow way goes left. You just stay on the ridgeline all the way. You'll be halfway there before this Smithers thinks twice, if he thinks at all."

"Thanks," I said.

"You two federal agents?" he asked.

"No," I said, going out.

Beyond the door was a small plank bridge that crossed a stream which wound down the hillside. Next to the stream, a rocky path rose up. At the top of the path, I took the trail to the left, as directed.

Trying to make as little noise as possible, I crossed the ridge, stopping now and then to catch the sound of any pursuer. At first, I couldn't hear a thing except my own breathing, but then my imagination got the better of me and I hurried on. After a time, I was sure I'd either lost Smithers, or he was still standing outside the stable like the dangerous idiot he appeared to be.

Finally, the lights of the company houses appeared below me. I sat on my haunches, surveying the street, and caught my breath. Satisfied no one was around, I inched downhill through the bushes until I was catty-cornered from the house.

I felt safer when the door swung open and I saw Kayce Powell.

13

"This is Bill Edmonson," Kayce Powell told the ruddy-complected fine-boned man with thick red hair who was sitting at the table in the center of the room.

"We weren't so sure you'd come," said the man, standing up and holding out his hand.

"Why?" I asked. "How could I pass up such a tempting invitation?" I shook his hand and took the same chair I had the night before.

"Kayce told me about you and Frank Grant last night. Then we heard what happened to Frank."

"What'd you hear?"

"Just that they found his body in a coal car in Wild Stream."

"That's all I got out of Sheriff Chaney, too."

"Chaney's an asshole."

"You'll get no argument out of me. I can't say much for his choice of deputies, either. Smithers has been following me."

The man motioned Kayce Powell toward the door.

"He isn't out there," I said. "I lost him."

"You better be right. These miners are putting their lives on the line in dealing with me."

"Then you're the union organizer that Briggs and Chaney are so worried about?"

He nodded. "That bunch'll tell you I'm a Bolshevik with a bomb in my pocket and shrunken baby heads hanging from my belt. Others'll tell you I helped them get a better wage. That's why they trust me. That's why Kayce and the others keep me informed about what's going on."

"I didn't get your name."

"Stephen O'Dell." He ran his hand through his red hair before he asked, "Why'd you and Frank Grant come to town?"

"That question seems to be on everyone's lips," I said. Then I launched into the tried-and-true cover story.

O'Dell cut me off somewhere in the middle of Child's ballad exploits. "Why the hell would a private detective like Frank Grant suddenly turn into a ballad scholar?"

"I don't know what you're talking about," I said. "I only met the professor a few months ago."

"Yeah? What if I told you I knew him a long time. Or that we were in the same town at the same time more than once. Why don't you try again? Why did you guys come to Blind Spring?"

"I told you. We were after old stories."

"Well, Frank always did like old stories, didn't he? Last time I ran into him was on a train the night a railroad strike started. We had to thumb a ride west on a canal boat. He said he was after 'old stories' then, too. When the truth finally came out, I had some information he was able to use. Maybe I can help you."

There was little doubt that this Stephen O'Dell had known Grant. Probably much better than I had. Grant had told me the same tale on the train.

"Maybe you *can* help me," I said.

O'Dell smiled, showing some missing teeth. "Who are you working for?"

A crock of good the folklore cover was doing me. Even Ben McGraw had seen through it. And now I was faced with a question I couldn't answer. But at least O'Dell didn't seem to know the answer either.

"You know that's confidential," I said, trying not to show my ignorance.

"Then what's the case? I figure it has to do with that prospector's death five years ago. Kayce says you guys brought up Gatini last night."

"There are people who don't think the Italian killed Lancelot Scott," I said. "Of course, you must know they took Gatini to the pen yesterday."

"Ahead of time, too," said O'Dell. "That must have thrown Frank. He probably figured you'd have at least a few days to work on the thing before they shipped Gatini out."

"You keep track of what happens in town, don't you?"

"Have to. That's *my* business. I know all sorts of things, like the fact you visited Timothy Briggs this afternoon."

"How'd you find that out?"

"I told you. The people who want to see changes keep me informed." He lifted a glass from the table and took a long drink. "Some whiskey?"

"No, thanks." I didn't want to worry about the whiskey hitting my near-empty, nervous stomach on top of everything else.

"Frank Grant never turned down whiskey," he said. "He could be a rough bastard, but I liked him. I can be a rough bastard myself. How'd you size up Briggs?"

"I wouldn't want to be in your shoes and have to negotiate with him. You like rough bastards, I think he's right up your alley."

"Look, you don't have to play your cards so close to your chest. Maybe we can work together, like Frank and I did sometimes. The way I see it, you can use all the help you can get.

Some kid comes to town playing assistant to the professor, and the professor gets bumped off. You don't envy me negotiating with Briggs, I don't envy you on your own against the sheriff and the mine guards. If you want to play spoiled brat, you can hop on the next train heading east. It ain't going to get easier. But, if we team up, we might find some answers. Any dirt you dig up on Briggs and Chaney can't hurt our side. And, just like you, I want to find out who murdered Frank. There's bound to be some murmurs about what happened. I know plenty of miners with ears. Likewise, a lot of the miners knew Gatini."

"Look, I'm not trying to be difficult, but we don't have the same thing in mind. I want to find out who killed Grant. If Briggs and Chaney have something to do with it, then that's the way it is. As far as Gatini goes, if you know miners who can help clear him, then why don't they come forth?"

"I saw Chaney and Kirk arrest him last fall," said Kayce Powell. I'd almost forgotten there was anyone else in the room.

"They came to the mines?"

"To the East Works. I don't think Alberto knew why he was being arrested. He'd never bothered to learn much English, so none of the other miners knew him too well. We heard he laid in his cell at night and cried, not knowing what it was all about. They kept him here, instead of the county seat, so Chaney could keep an eye on him."

"So you think he's innocent?" I asked.

"I don't see how he could have killed anyone. Of course, the whole thing happened before most of us came to Blind Spring."

"They put the Italian on trial at the worst possible time," said O'Dell. "The newspapers were filled with accounts of the trials resulting from the Logan County miners' march. They say Briggs' prosecutor went into a spiel about Italian anarchists and how this country was going to the dogs. The jury didn't take long to decide, I'm told. You've seen enough of this town to know how it works, Edmonson. That's why I can't believe you won't work with us. Frank wouldn't sit there twiddling his thumbs. Briggs and Chaney and the rest of them deserve all the trouble we can give them. If we can chop down the guys who run this town, I intend to. I'm here to help the miners."

O'Dell's staring eyes were almost hypnotic. It didn't take much imagination to picture the impact he'd have on small, secret gatherings of coal miners. Maybe I *was* being bull-headed about not throwing in my lot with him, but . . . how do you say it? I wasn't comfortable about it. I just didn't like him. *Hell.*

"I keep telling you. I want to find a murderer, no matter who he is. Maybe two murderers. You're out to organize for John L. Lewis. Everything's not so black and white," I said.

O'Dell rubbed at his thin nose. It was slightly lopsided, as if it had once been broken. "You're dense, Edmonson. Haven't you breathed enough of the air here? Don't you see what the miners have to put up with?"

"The conditions aren't ones I'd want to live with," I said.

"Things have gotten worse in this state since the Logan coal war. But we can't give up. Union miners in Pennsylvania and other parts of West Virginia earn seven and a half dollars a day. Briggs pays less than five, the going rate before the war. He's right up Harding's alley. When Warren G. spouts his idiocy about a return to normalcy, what he means is returning wages to the old days. They're doing that right now to the railroad workers. If the union wage is cut back to five dollars a day, what will the unorganized workers get? You think Timothy Briggs is going to lower the prices at his company stores? Will he reduce the rent on these company houses?"

O'Dell's voice was arching into a holy roller revivalist's hellfire and brimstone. "Hell, Briggs'll rob these miners and their families more than he's robbing them now. They might as well be slaves or indentured servants like in the olden days. I'm asking you to help us. We'll return the favor. Together we might be able to blow this town so high and far that it'll come down in the real America."

"I'll think about it," I said, pushing back from the table and standing up. As I walked across the room, I saw Kayce Powell leaning against the doorframe, his face a blank white mask. I tried to smile.

O'Dell called to me in a lower, wearier voice. "Don't tell anyone about tonight, or about me."

I realized he was as scared as I was. He'd showed his hand and I hadn't signed on. He didn't know much about me, except that I'd come to town with Grant. He didn't know whether I'd run straight back to the *District of Columbia* and let the old man know what he'd said. But O'Dell did know there were plenty of towns where he could get lynched for saying less than he had in the last hour.

Powell moved, and I reached for the doorknob. Turning back, I said, "Don't worry. I don't come from a family of millionaires. I wish you luck."

Outside, I glanced up and down the street before stepping off the porch. It was as quiet as it had been when I'd arrived. I hadn't gone more than a block, however, before the silence was assaulted.

"*. . . railroad . . . lose . . . wife . . .*" He came nearer and nearer, repeating his odd chant. "*Jesus Christ . . . great . . . lose . . . railroad . . . lose your wife . . .*"

"Evening, Harry," I said as we passed.

"Think you're great?" His face was so close I could smell his whiskey breath. "Only Jesus Christ was great. Lose your railroad."

I walked on, and so did he. The farther away he got, the more his words became distorted, slurred by alcohol through the dark and distance, until it sounded like he was moaning, "Onee Jesus cry was great, lose your bail load, lose yore why, tink yore gray."

I was glad when I was out of earshot and alone again. There were things worse than being alone, no matter what Stephen O'Dell thought.

14

Simpson the singing bellhop rapped on my door while I was dressing on Saturday morning. He handed me the telegram, then hurried off down the hall.

The boss had been just as careful with his wording as I'd been with mine. He must have known my communications with the agency weren't necessarily private. All he'd wired was: GRANT'S BODY TAKEN CARE OF. KEEP WORKING.

Easy to command from a New York office.

Easy for him to pretend I knew what I was doing.

Of course, what I planned to do was the only thing I could think to do. I figured I would start by retracing Grant's steps on Thursday, the day he'd been killed. The places he'd visited, like the widow's, had to have something to do with Gatini and the prospector, and those same places might have something to do with what had happened to Grant. Such was my theory, at least.

Keep working. I suppose my mind was. In the hotel's dining room, over breakfast, I found myself solving one mystery. A tiny one, but a beginning nevertheless. It could be I was dense, as Stephen O'Dell had accused, but it wasn't until I sat watching the waiters come and go that it dawned on me there was more than one way out of the Briggs Hotel. Grant hadn't meticulously checked "the lay of the land" on Thursday for nothing. When we'd circled the building on our arrival, he'd noted the kitchen door where the fellow was peeling potatoes. So, later that night, there'd been no need for him to tangle with the deputy guarding the front porch. He had simply ducked out the back and gone his way, wherever that was.

Christ. Was I starting to think like Frank Grant?

But where had he gone?

Keep working.

"What's the widow's name again, and how do I get to her house?" I asked Ben McGraw as soon as I entered the stable.

"Susannah Chester, but everyone calls her Suze," he said as he led me back to a stall. While he saddled the horse, McGraw furnished directions as clear as could be expected.

"You work for the governor?" he asked as I climbed into the saddle.

"No."

I didn't bother to remind him I was a folklore collector. I guessed the cover had become one I'd slip on when I really needed it, and slip off when it wasn't much use. With McGraw, as with O'Dell and Powell, it no longer seemed to matter.

I rode out the back door of the stable and up the steep hill I'd hiked the night before. When I reached the top, I stopped and looked back on Blind Spring. It was hard to believe I'd only spent two nights in town. Just two mornings before, Grant and I had climbed off the train. I already felt like I'd overstayed my welcome.

Through the foliage, I could see some rooves on an upper residential street and, below them, the formidable Briggs Hotel. Further away, I could see the rooftops of store buildings on Briggs Boulevard, bits of the Shawnee–Potomac tracks, and the cupola of the station house. The clouds of recent days were sliding northeast, freeing the summer sky.

Straight down the rise, I could just about make out the gasoline station in front of McGraw's stable. Feeling strange being on horseback in these days of motor cars, I guided the horse away from the company houses and up into the mountains that appeared so dangerous to Briggs Junior and Dr. Corman.

Now and then, I passed narrow side trails that corkscrewed up the ridges around me. As McGraw had directed, I stayed to the main road, ignoring the smaller ones, though they made me understand why Grant had insisted on horses. There were still places in this part of the country where a car was more trouble than it was worth.

The morning sun was starting to fry the mountainside by the time I got to the old farm road. Turning left, I picked up the pace. The motion of the horse began to relax me. It felt good to get away from Blind Spring for the day, good to be finally about business, even if I wasn't sure of the business.

I never had been good at puzzles. My mother would bring them home, but I'd always end up leaving them to her and my sisters once I saw how hard they were. I was more inclined to go to the movies or play baseball.

I came to the burned-out house. McGraw had warned me to keep my eyes open for it, and I spotted it in spite of the tangle of brush nearly covering the foundation stones. I turned left again, up a wagon-rutted road that ran deeper into the mountains.

The wagon road seemed very old, the kind my grandfather in Virginia had called a "dug" road to distinguish it from a "grade" road. I sensed the road had been there long before Timothy Briggs, long before the scramble for coal; maybe even long before the United States of America. Horses had trampled it for generations. I felt as if I were diving back through time, as if time itself was as collectable as those damn ballads of Grant's.

The horse was well-trained and the route wasn't as imposing as it had looked at first. It was easy to ride along and let my head float elsewhere. All new to me, this world. No mother, no sisters, no coeds, no teachers, no classrooms. No Grant.

Had I been right to steer clear of Stephen O'Dell?

I told myself yes. I didn't need his baggage weighing me down. I had plenty of my own.

Keep working.

Goddamn right, boss.

I came to the field dotted with roaming cattle, then the collapsed cabin, then the white frame church that McGraw had described. Two women carrying buckets and rags were walking down the road. I called to them before they turned up the path to the church.

"Which house is Suze Chester's?"

The older of the two pointed in the direction of a large frame farmhouse that nestled against a hill about a quarter of a mile away. I felt my nervousness taking over as I rode closer. The tightness got worse as I climbed down and tied the horse to a post in front of a barn that was partly dug into the mountainside. Slowly, I walked to the porch.

Every muscle in me seemed to lock when I saw the fellow by the door. He was leaned back on a swing, his legs stretched out in front of him. He looked in his forties and wore much-patched overalls, with no shirt beneath them and a dented-up hat on his head. But he didn't challenge me. With each of his snores, his mustache moved and the swing swayed. He didn't even stir when I went up the steps to the door.

Suze Chester turned out to be more alert. "What do you want?" she demanded before I'd raised my hand to knock.

I squinted through the screen door, but couldn't see her.

"My name's Bill Edmonson. Frank Grant is dead."

15

"Terrible about Grant," said Suze Chester. "Of course, I only met him the once, but I was hoping he'd dig out the truth about what happened to Scott."

Ham sizzled in the skillet. Green beans bubbled in the pot. The heat of the woodstove on the hot day made her kitchen seem stifling and closed-in. Even the shadowy corners behind the cupboard and the home-sawed shelves of jars didn't look cool, only dark.

"So Grant told you why we came to town?"

She nodded as she walked toward me and put the plates on the table. "And he told me about you, too. Believe me, I wouldn't be talking to you otherwise. He said he'd come back one day with his assistant, Bill Edmonson. I remembered the name. I thought the two of you might be back today or tomorrow for a trip to Scott's mine."

"I wish Grant hadn't left me back in the hotel when he came up here Thursday afternoon. If I'd been with him, I might know exactly what was on his mind, instead of having to second-guess and reconstruct everything he did on the day he died."

Like a schoolteacher, Suze corrected me. "You mean, everything he did on the day he was *murdered*. Just like Scott was murdered. Somebody didn't want neither of them around. Briggs and Chaney always change the world to their liking."

Her voice had a hollow sound, like she formed her words in the roof of her mouth and didn't let them stray far from her lips just in case she wanted to recall them. But she wasn't recalling them now.

"So you think Briggs and Chaney had something to do with both Scott's death and Grant's?" I asked.

"I'm starting to believe they have something to do with nearly everything. And I don't like it, or them, one bit. Do I believe they stuck an axe in Scott's chest? I can't prove it. Chaney was in the army five years ago, and Briggs hadn't moved here yet, but his agents were around."

"His agents?"

"Men scouting land for him."

"How about Chaney's top deputies? There's one named Smithers."

"Never heard of him."

"The chief deputy's named Josh Kirk."

"Kirk grew up on the east end of the county, so I didn't know him or his folks well. But, from what I've heard, he was away in the war when Scott was murdered, too. I don't know most of those men that are mine guards. They came after Briggs came."

"What did Grant want to know when he came up here?" I asked.

"It was the middle of the afternoon. I was picking strawberries. He climbed down off his horse and stuttered around a few minutes with a bunch of *Nice day, ma'am*'s. You could tell there was something on his mind. He said he was collecting old songs and stories, and we must have chatted half an hour before he mentioned Scott. The minute he did, I asked him if he was working for Briggs or for the law. I told him he'd better have clean hands to shake mine. He was probably sizing me up, too.

Before long, he came out with it, that you two were detectives. He wanted to know if I believed Alberto really murdered Scott."

"Did he?"

"Didn't you get my meaning earlier?" Her eyes lighted on me then, and I sensed a sadness folded into the lines of her face. "I'd be blaming it on someone else."

"Did Grant tell you everything—who we were working for and all?"

"No, but I'd have hired you myself if I'd known I could. I wrote the governor once, but he never answered. Who *are* you working for?"

Well, it had seemed smart to ask her what she knew about our employer, even if the question had backfired. I tried changing the subject, and she let me get away with it.

"What'd you tell Grant about Lancelot Scott's murder?" I asked.

"Just what I knew. After an hour or two, he said he had to get back to town. He told me not to tell anyone he'd been here, and that he'd be back with you. He wanted me to take the pair of you to the mine where Scott was killed."

"But what did you tell him about Scott?"

"Scott lived here while he was prospecting. It's a big house. Ever since my husband died and the kids went to Ohio for jobs, I've always taken in boarders, rented out rooms. Not that there's many boarders to take in, you understand. There's some hunters now and then, a few folks traveling the mountains, a prospector or two like Scott. He hated the name Lancelot, you know. Detested it. Said he'd rather have been called Gertrude." She laughed, and it registered on me that she was reliving some memory. "Scott was funny like that. Eccentric, I guess you'd call him. Oh, he could be funny and charming. He could charm the pants off a nun. He could convince you to go to hell with him. He'd grin and say, 'No wood to chop in hell. Fire burns all the time without tending. You can rub shoulders with a lot of fine people, and the preachers have given up preaching so they aren't recognized.'"

She laughed again, but, as she turned back to the stove, I thought she was sobbing.

When I felt the asking was safe, I tossed out another question. "Where was Scott from?"

"He'd been all over, from New England to the West Coast. Stayed a time in Texas as a cowboy. That's where he gave up the name Lancelot for good. He came to America from Scotland in his teens. From Glasgow. Said his father was a Scotsman and his mother was French. Somewhere out West he worked for a mining concern. That's where he got the notion to strike out on his own. He was getting on, and beginning to worry about his old age. He was around fifty when he came here, just a year or two older than me."

"Why'd he pick these parts?"

"He'd studied mining books and geology reports, and found there was coal and maybe iron around Blind Spring, but no one had ever made a go of it because there was always water in the mines. He figured it was worth a try, mainly because he had the place to himself and it was close to Pittsburgh and Eastern cities. He had a side to him like that, a real smart business side."

"How long did he board with you?"

"Six years."

"That's a long time to live with someone."

"Or not long enough," she said, placing a platter of ham on the table in front of me.

"Did you tell Grant anything else?"

"I suggested he look up John Summerset."

"Who's John Summerset?"

"He's the one found Scott's body. They drank together. I wouldn't let Scott drink here, so he'd go over to Summerset's place once in a while. I don't approve of drinking, but Scott grew up on whiskey. The Summerset clan have always made homebrew. He sells to miners and timbermen."

It clicked. That was why Grant had been looking for the whiskey man on Thursday night, why he'd been careful to let the bootlegger know we weren't still-busters.

"I guess I'll go see John Summerset," I said. "Is he the one they call the whiskey man down in town?"

"They call them all the whiskey man, but he's one of them."

She carried a bowl of green beans to the table. A moment later, she was back with hot rolls. Then she wiped her stubby fingers on her apron, crossed to the door, and went out on the porch. Soon she was back, followed by the tall fellow with the long mustaches. Still half-asleep, he rubbed at his eyes. When he saw me, he seemed surprised as hell, but he just sat across the round table from me and stared.

Suze untied her apron, dropped it over the back of a chair, and joined us. "It's hot," she said, the back of her hand brushing at her gray-streaked hair. "Take your suitcoat off. There's limits to being gentlemanly. You're in the hills now."

As I hung my coat over the back of the cane-bottomed chair, I considered removing the awkward holster, too. But I didn't, and Suze didn't mention the gun. Still, I could feel the other man's eyes on me.

"What do *you* believe happened to Grant?" asked Suze, breaking the quiet.

I stopped cutting the slice of ham. "Other than being buried in a coal car, I have no idea." I glanced over at the man from the swing. He was busy buttering a roll and didn't appear to be paying us much mind.

"Don't worry about Moses," said Suze, sensing my nervousness. "He couldn't hear the thunder and lightning if it drove him in the mud. He's deaf."

She said the word the old way, like my grandfather had. *Deef*. At least, I grasped why my entrance hadn't aroused him, why she'd had to go out to bring him in to eat, why she wasn't concerned about our table talk.

"Does Moses live here?" I asked.

She nodded, then corrected herself. "He didn't live here when Scott did. He's come since. You need a man around a farm like this. Need someone for chores. Moses doesn't have anyone. He never did hear good and, after he worked dynamiting tunnels for the Shawnee–Potomac, he couldn't hear at all. He doesn't bother to talk much anymore, either. He was living in a shack, not far from where the hotel is, when Briggs bought up the town. He was sort of a squatter, so he had to find someplace to live fast."

"Did he meet Grant the other day?"

"No. He'd gone down to town that morning to sell strawberries and run errands for me. He didn't come back until night. I doubt if he and Grant even passed on the road."

Moses began staring at me again, like he knew we were talking about him.

"It's your gun," explained Suze. "He likes your gun. He likes revolvers. If you want to make a friend, you'll let him shoot it after dinner."

"I obviously need all the friends I can get," I answered.

Suze shot a bunch of hand signals to Moses. At one point, she pointed to the pistol in my shoulder holster and he gave a smile. After that, he ate hurriedly, cutting his ham with quick strokes and carting the beans from his plate to his mouth. When he was done, he nodded at Suze, screeched his chair back across the planked floor, and went outside.

"He'll be waiting on you," she told me.

"I don't have to eat that fast, do I?"

She laughed. "Take your time. He's like a little kid. He'll grumble, but he'll wait."

"After I let him shoot a while, what if we go see the place

where Scott was killed? You said you were expecting to take Grant and me there."

"Don't see why not," she said, lifting her plate and taking it over to the sink. "I'll redd up while you're out with Moses."

It occurred to me that, like my mother, Suze Chester wouldn't go anyplace until the dishes were all washed and the chores were all done. What was important depended on the person deciding the importance. She must have been a stiff antidote for Scott's eccentricity, and he must have been a good cure for her mountain-widow loneliness. For a minute, I watched her at the sink, where a handpump had been rigged up to create some semblance of indoor plumbing. Then I went searching for Moses.

He wasn't on the porch, but, by the time I'd gotten down the steps, he'd showed up from around the house. He led me back the way I guessed he'd come, past a fruit-cellar basement, past a corncrib with cracked ribs, along a worn footpath that curved around a hogpen where our dinner ham had probably been raised.

Moses stopped near a smokehouse and pointed to a piece of brown pasteboard nailed to a fencepost. I took the gun from my holster and handed it over. He studied the weapon a while, turning it over and over in his large bony hand. Then he aimed.

I jumped at the loudness of the shot, and hoped Moses hadn't noticed. The bullet missed the piece of pasteboard altogether and ripped through a bush off to the right. Then he gave me the gun.

So, we'd be having a shooting contest. I never had claimed to be a great shot, hadn't grown up with a six-gun in my hand. Never had shot a man. Grant had led me through a little target practice, and that was about it.

I aimed, pulled the trigger, and managed to hit the fencepost below the mark. If the target had been a man, I'd have hit him in the balls. Messy, but effective.

I returned the pistol to Moses. His second shot seemed to graze the edge of the target, leaving the pasteboard shaking.

I took the gun back and tried to correct my aim. The bullet tore across the top of the post, splintering the locust pole a fraction of an inch above the target.

A man's neck, maybe.

Before I surrendered the gun, I shot again without thinking.

A heart, perhaps.

When I saw Moses' eyes flash, I knew I was through for the day. No sense pushing my luck.

He shot again and hit what would have been the right lung, which seemed to satisfy him as we made our way back around the house.

Suze was over by the barn hitching horses to a small wagon. Moses fell into helping her, and when they were finished, she telegraphed another series of hand signs to him.

"I told him to water your horse," she said as we climbed up to the seat. She pointed back to the wagon bed. "I brought along your coat, in case you want it."

Despite the afternoon heat, I reached for it. I didn't want passersby wondering about my gun.

16

Summer-thick brambles lined the trail. Thorns snatched at my coat sleeves. Insects flew around my eyes. The way was so narrow that it could have been a deer path, and the trees were so heavy with leaves that the afternoon had become almost like dusk.

"It's grown up in the last five years, since Scott died," said Suze Chester, like she had read my mind. She'd said it wasn't far when we'd left the wagon and started down the hill, but I was beginning to feel like we were characters in some French-and-Indian-War saga.

Suze was an unlikely guide. Six inches shorter than I, and twice as round, she almost waddled down the path. As she rolled ahead, she ignored bugs, stickers, and any threat of snakes.

Somehow I'd expected Scott's mine would be the center of much activity. I guess I'd pictured it being taken over by Briggs and Company, but that didn't turn out to be the case. In fact, I was surprised when Suze slowed down and said, "This is it." Little more than a clearing, you could have easily missed it.

"Doesn't really look like much today, does it? You'd never

believe Scott poured every penny he could rake up into this hole. He never got the retirement nest egg he hoped for."

"I don't even see the hole," I said.

She took a few more steps and pointed to the edge of the woods. "There's the shaft. You can sort of make it out."

"Sort of. How come it's been filled in? Wasn't there coal here? Why didn't Briggs just take it over?"

"Oh, there was some coal. It was supposed to be semi-anthracite, somewhere between hard and soft coal. It should have been sellable. I've always guessed Briggs thought it poor taste to use Scott's mine. It would have added to the rumors that he killed Scott so he could move in."

"You're probably right. Where's Briggs' mine?"

"Further down the hill. We'll go there in a bit. There's a place you can see it from. They say the seam is thicker there, and it doesn't have the water problem that always nagged Scott. Besides, Briggs' mine is closer to the valley. They've timbered a road up and down, and there's a spur line of the railroad running right to it. No telling what Scott could have done if he'd gotten the Shawnee–Potomac to cooperate. That was always his hope."

I followed her over to the onetime mine shaft. "This used to be a tram line," she said. "The tram cost Scott a bundle. May have been what broke him. But he didn't know how else to get the coal out. He had a couple mules to haul the tram. Briggs filled in the shaft and took anything he could use."

Looking around, I tried to picture the site as it had been in 1918. "Did Scott ever sell coal?"

"Just a little, here and there. Mostly he dug and showed the place off to people he thought could help him raise money. I remember one man who accused him of buying coal and spreading it around the mine to make it look like it was a good prospect." She laughed again. "Of course, Scott wasn't guilty, but I wouldn't have put it past him. Sometimes, he'd send samples to an assayer. I don't remember his name, but he's the one decided it was somewhere between anthracite and bituminous."

"Then, mostly he was just trying to get financing and drum up interest?"

She nodded. "He was always talking about *capital*, about attracting a capitalist. I guess he finally attracted one."

"Do you remember any of the people he tried to interest?"

"Not offhand. He didn't tell me al the ins and outs of the business. Some of his papers are up in my attic. I could go through them if you want."

"Couldn't hurt. If you find anything, Ben McGraw'll know where to get me."

"Of course, I don't know who might have contacted Charlie about the land."

"Charlie?"

"Charlie Happersalk. He owned this hillside, and the spot where Briggs' mine is now, too."

"Is he still around?"

"No. He died a year or so after the war. By then, he'd moved to California to live with his son. I don't think he'd ever have sold the land so long as Scott was alive."

"They had some kind of deal about the mine?"

"Scott and Charlie had a written agreement that Scott had rights to dig, and Charlie'd get a percentage of any profits. Scott was wise in his own way, like I told you. He always insisted on getting everything down in writing. I was a distant cousin of Charlie Happersalk's, which, I guess, is one reason he and Scott got together on it. I always felt it was Scott's insistence on a written contract that did him in."

"What do you mean?"

"Charlie took the paper as serious as Scott did. If the powers that be could just have found a way to evict Scott and taken over the mountain, he might still be alive."

"Did the whiskey man—did John Summerset find the body here at the shaft?"

Suze pointed up the hill, through brush and young trees, at a spot deeper into the woods. Squinting, I could make out the shape of two log buildings almost lost in the growth. She circled around the filled-in shaft and started toward the cabins. We hadn't gone ten feet before I stepped in a hole and fell.

"Watch yourself," she said. "There's prospect pits all over. Scott was always digging for something. He was always hoping for good coal, or iron ore, or something. He used to sit at the table at night and tell me how western Virginia had lots of iron bloomeries in the old days, before they found the fine red ore in Michigan. I used to love to hear him talk his head off about ore and prospecting, but the mining itself always scared me. I always feared his little mine wasn't safe. Men die in big mines all the time, you know. I always think of their women, afraid every time the whistle blows. I told Scott I didn't want him to be a big mine boss, but he said it was better to be a boss than to be a miner."

She stopped by the first of the log structures. "This was Scott's office and storeroom." The door was leaning off its hinges, and the single room was empty except for a wooden bunk. "Anything usable's been taken by now. Scott slept here when he'd stay overnight."

"Then this is where Summerset found him?"

Again, Suze Chester pointed further into the woods. "He was found laying over there, his own axe in him. I'd come looking for him, but I hadn't gone far from the buildings. It wasn't unusual for him to disappear for days without telling anyone. He'd make a trip to the courthouse to read a deed, or go over to Summerset's for some whiskey, or just light off into the mountains to dig more prospect pits. He was a free soul. So, anyway, when I got here and didn't see him, I assumed he was just off somewheres. He'd had me worried before. . . ."

Her voice was tailing into sadness. As we stared into the empty cabin, I began to feel the same way myself. There was something haunted, or haunting, about the site.

"What's the other building?" I asked.

"That one was for the miners. But he only had the one—Alberto Gatini."

As we walked to the other structure, I asked, "Was Gatini here when you came looking for Scott?"

"No, Scott had given him a couple weeks off to save paying his wages."

"How long had Gatini been working for Scott?" I asked, looking into the empty bunkhouse. It was almost identical to Scott's own cabin.

"A little over a year. Scott had gone to the city to see about some money and, when he came back, he had Alberto with him."

"I take it they got along."

"Never saw any bad blood between them. Scott really liked the Italian, though it was funny to see them try to talk. They'd make signs, like you'd be talking to Moses, and then would come an English word or two, and they both knew a little French. No one else could have understood them."

"Where did Gatini go when he wasn't here? Where would he have gone when Scott gave him the time off?"

"Oh, he was right down in town. Of course, Blind Spring was much smaller in those days."

"And he lived in town after Scott was murdered?"

"He lived there right up till his arrest. In the summer of 1919, just when Briggs was starting up, Alberto got a job. I didn't keep track of him after that. I hadn't seen him for a year or more when I heard they'd framed him."

"Were you a witness at the trial?"

"Yes, but not what you'd call a main one. They asked me what Scott was like, his habits and all. They asked if I'd ever seen him and Alberto argue. I tried to say good things about Alberto, but I didn't know much. I wasn't at the mine every day. A few of the miners he worked with later, they testified for him, but no one could help him."

"Who was the main witness against him?"

"Wasn't one." Her eyes ran over the mine site. "How could there have been?"

"Ben McGraw says Gatini's attorney was next to worthless."

"That'd be fair. And the prosecutor Briggs hired was hell on wheels. He gave a big speech, reminding the jury how a foreigner tossed a bomb to start the Haymarket Riot in Chicago thirty or forty years ago, and he threw in about Sacco and Vanzetti, and about some Italian miner who sneaked up on Governor Cornwell at a union meeting in 1919. Alberto never had a chance."

She stopped talking and seemed so sad I thought she might cry, but then she straightened up. "You want to see the Briggs mine or not?"

"Sure."

We headed down the hill, past more of Scott's prospect pits. Whatever his faults, carelessness wasn't one of them—the man had been over every inch of the mountain. When we came to a small stream, Suze stared down at the summer-thin trickle.

"We found his shoe here once. He hadn't come home for a week, and I went looking for him, and I found his shoe here. Scott had been crossing the creek, his heel had stuck in the mud, and he'd walked right out of it and kept going. I guess that's why I didn't worry every time he didn't come home when I thought he should."

She lifted her long skirt and stepped over the stream, then trudged on silently. Finally, she came to a halt on a rocky ledge that overlooked a wide hollow.

"Over there," she pointed. "Briggs' West Works."

Across the hollow from us, two shafts had been sunk into the mountain. Their mouths were each three times bigger than Scott's shaft had been. Rails ran from the black holes to a huge factory-like building that squatted over a string of coal cars stretched along the tracks beneath. I knew enough about mining to know the building was the tipple, where the coal was sorted before being dumped into railroad cars.

"Scott could never have imagined all this," said Suze.

I was having enough trouble imagining it, and I was standing right there. The immensity of large industrial operations had always amazed me, and to find such an enterprise almost hidden in a mountain valley was all the more amazing. Not only was the landscape changed to fit the demands of industry, but the tipple and other buildings were designed to fit the landscape. They were interlocked, but not always lovingly.

"This isn't where Gatini worked, is it?" I asked after a while.

"He was at the East Works, on the other side of town."

"That's right," I said, remembering Kayce Powell saying he'd been at the East Works when the authorities had come to get the Italian.

"They say the East Works aren't much different than here," said Suze. "If anything, the East Works are bigger than this. The terrain's not as rough over there."

My eyes scanned the mining area and came to rest on a railroad car being loaded with coal from the tipple. Tons of black rock were crashing down. If a man—*if Grant*—had been in the car, he'd have been smashed, God, crushed beyond recognition.

I followed the line of cars with my eyes. The tracks ran down the hill as far as I could see, latching up somewhere with the Shawnee–Potomac mainline. On the hill below the mines, men were cutting what timber was left. Three or four trucks were coming up the road, through the timbered area.

"They're about to change shifts," said Suze like she'd watched it all before. I wondered how often she came there.

The trucks stopped near a frame building and dozens of men climbed down. Soon, those men were joined by others who'd been sitting on the hillside. I could see more men making their way up the road on foot.

The miners lined up outside the frame building and began filing in one door, then out another. I guessed they were signing in, clocking in, however it was that Briggs kept track of his miners' time.

From our distance, I couldn't see the expressions on the men's faces. They all had caps and lanterns, and dinnerpails in their hands. Then I noticed some of the hands, some of the faces, were black. Apparently, not all of the Negroes in Blind Spring were hotel workers and railroad porters. They were miners too, and there were Italian miners like Gatini, Welsh ones like Powell, mountaineers seeking a steady wage, and probably all manner of others, all come together at the Briggs mines to dig out a living.

Now, they filed to the mouth of a shaft. A man stood there, the sun bouncing off the deputy's badge on his chest, the mine guard's badge.

Before long, a small locomotive chugged out of the hole in the mountain, pulling a row of carts with miners in them. The men just finishing their shift were as black as minstrel showmen. I couldn't begin to tell who was really black and who was white, but I could imagine all of them blinking their eyes to adjust to the light after their hours underground.

The men climbed out of the carts and filed toward the wooden building. Soon, they were stepping up into truckbeds or walking down the hill. Their dinnerpails looked heavy in their hands. The new team of miners climbed aboard the carts, and, when they were all on, the small train again disappeared into the black mouth.

"It eats them," said Suze. "I told you I can't help but think of their women. You can't pay people enough to do that. They deserve whatever they can beg, borrow, or steal from the mine operators. It always ends bad, like a tunnel caving in, or Scott getting murdered."

She turned away from the mine and began walking slowly back the way we'd come.

What if Scott had made a success of it? I wondered. Whose side would Suze be on if he'd made a million and become the big mine boss instead of Timothy Briggs?

But, for all his sweat, all his digging, all his blood, Scott hadn't made a success of it.

Most men didn't.

17

Suze didn't speak as we rode back to her house. The afternoon's talk, the tour of the mines, the dislodged memories of Scott had obviously done her in. Climbing down from the wagon, she insisted on feeding me again, and went straight to her kitchen, leaving Moses and me to unhitch the horses.

When I walked in the house, she was cutting ham and warming up the green beans left over from the midday meal. Sitting in the middle of the round table was a treasure she'd hauled out to show me.

"That's Scott," she announced.

I picked up the framed photograph. Lancelot Scott appeared to be a tall, solid man, though not big enough to stop a swinging axe and remain unscathed. The picture must have been taken on a fall day. The leaves were off the trees and the area around his mine shaft was cleared and incredibly bare, not at all as it had looked just a while before. He was leaning on a gnarled walking stick, its point resting in a pile of his prized product, his coal, and he wore heavy trousers with dirt-smudged knees and a tweed jacket that looked like it had been caught on ten thousand stickers. His hair was closely cropped, and, sitting high on his head, was a tam, one of those round Scottish caps.

"What's so funny?" asked Suze as she put a ham sandwich in front of me. She must have heard my quiet chuckle.

"The hat. I just find it odd for a man to be wandering around West Virginia in a hat like that."

"He had his ways. He had a whole collection of hats—from each place he'd been—cowboy hats, baseball caps, a miner's helmet, even a beret. They're still upstairs. He'd wear a different topper every day to fit his mood. And you should have heard how he could talk. He still had a bit of a brogue, or whatever you call it. It was wonderful to hear him, full of himself and all his dreams. This is America, he'd say, where a man can make his fortune. He wasn't like no one else that ever was around here."

Later, riding back to town, I kept imagining that picture of Scott at his mine in his tam and tweeds, with his walking stick and his cocky stance. He just might have been a match for Timothy Briggs, whose head was so big that his body might have withered in reaction.

I had to admit, the time spent with Suze Chester had captured my interest in who'd killed Scott. After all, we'd come to town to prove Alberto Gatini wasn't the one who'd stuck an axe in Scott's chest in 1918. But Grant's murder was still the main thing. At least I'd managed to fill in most of Grant's final day. If he'd ridden up to Suze's while I'd napped on Thursday afternoon, he couldn't have done much else. I'd been with him all morning and night. The only blank space was the late evening, after he'd ditched me at the hotel. So, if he hadn't returned to Suze's, where had he gone?

Dusk was falling as I rode down the old "dug" road. I'd just turned right at the burned-out house when my horse neighed and kicked up its front legs a little. As soon as I saw the snake crawling from among the foundation stones, I reached for my gun, ready for more target practice.

"Ain't worth the bullet."

The surprise voice brought me up short, and it took me a moment to figure out where it was coming from.

"Just a black snake," said the man as he came riding from the woods. His soft, flat voice was vaguely familiar, but I didn't recognize the skinny weathered face at all. "All snakes ain't killers," he said, drawing near. "Even a rattler's got the courtesy to rattle before it strikes. Not that you'd want to get bit by any snake, mind you, but you can't much fear the ones that ain't poison. Let them go their way. All bites ain't equal. The ones you got to be leery of are the mean, silent copperheads."

Watching the black snake slither away, I said, "I don't think I've had the pleasure."

"Ain't much pleasure involved. Might be less if you don't put that goddamn gun away. . . . That's friendlier," he said after I'd holstered the pistol. "Anyways, we've met, sort of. Name's John Summerset."

"That's what I guessed," I said, glancing at the baskets slung over the back of his saddle.

"Moses came over this afternoon and let me know you're wanting to talk to me."

At that, I understood what some of the signs between Suze and Moses had been about.

"You riding down to Blind Spring?" I asked.

"Yeah. Saturday night. Best business night of the week," he said, pulling a cigarette out of his pocket and lighting it. He gave his horse a gentle kick and started down the road.

"My name's Bill Edmonson," I told him. "Do you always have to dump your cargo like you did the other night when the deputies came? I've heard Chaney's boys are rough on whiskey men."

"They don't invite me to dances," said Summerset. "I've lost more than one load of brew. You got to be ready to get away quick. It's the only way a small operator can survive."

"You could carry your stuff better, and get away quicker, with a car."

"Hell, then I'd be pretty much stranded on the same roads the mine guards travel. You ain't that grabbed by the whiskey business, are you?"

"No. I suppose you've heard what happened to Frank Grant."

"Yeah, I heard about the professor, but I can't help you there. You saw when I left town the other night. I thought it was Scott's death you wanted to talk about. That's what Moses led me to believe."

"In my mind, it's all tied up. Everything that's happened here is one ball of string."

"I guess that's how you got to see it."

"Suze says you're the one who found Scott's body."

"Yeah."

"So tell me about it."

"I told all I know in court," said Summerset. "Scott had been gone a few days, and Suze sent word up to me, asking if he was there. Now, I liked Scott. Wasn't unusual for him to be at my place, but I hadn't seen him. So I went down to his mine and called around. Went up to the bunkhouse, too, even though I knew Alberto was gone all week. I don't know what it was made me take off through the weeds, but I did, and I come across the body. Awful sight, I won't forget. The axe in him, all that blood, him laying on the ground in the filth, the dog-days heat and maggots and worms and flies. I covered him with a blanket from Alberto's bunk and went and got a wagon and put the body on it and took him down to the station. They telegrammed for the sheriff—Paul Fuller in them days—and I never let Suze know till they'd carted the body away. Wasn't right for her to see Scott like that. She couldn't have stood it."

"You don't have any idea who killed him?"

"Oh, I got my notions, like all the old residenters do. Notions don't do no good, though, when the law's on the other side. Pinning it on someone's different than shooting the breeze."

"You don't think it was Gatini?"

"Hell, no. Ask anyone about him. He wasn't no killer. Christ, he never even complained about working in Briggs' mines. He was too damn timid, afraid he'd lose his job. Ask the Italian bakers about him."

"Why them?"

"That's where he lived. He rented a little room from them behind the Blind Spring Bakery."

I nodded to show I'd registered his suggestion. Then I tried another angle. "What I can't figure out about this conspiracy that some allege is that Timothy Briggs wasn't even in town yet, was he? And Chaney was off in the war. How could they have had something to do with Scott's death?"

"The hills was crawling with geologists and men from Philadelphia that summer. Briggs mightn't have been here in person, but he sure was here in spirit. Word was out that a rich man wanted to buy up all the land he could get his hands on. See, he wanted it all. He wasn't about to pay out cash for the east end of the mountain and not the west, for the valley and not the ridges. Scott had a big part of it tied up in his deal with Charlie Happersalk, and Scott wouldn't budge."

"You don't think Happersalk had anything to do with it, do you?"

"God, no. Not Charlie. He didn't give a damn about money, not even enough for his own good. He'd had chances to sell the land before Scott came along. Charlie only let the ridge be mined at all because Scott kept pestering him, and because Suze was some relative of his."

"But he sold out to Briggs in the end, didn't he?"

"Don't know all the details of that. By then, Scott was dead and Charlie was old, tired, and didn't have no family around here to give it to. Don't blame him. They all sold out, except for Ben McGraw and one or two others. The Philadelphia money was too green. Nobody'd seen anything like it before."

I remembered Dr. Corman's remark on the train, how dirt farmers were happy to sell family plots.

John Summerset reined his horse to a halt. "I take another route from here."

"There's nothing more you can tell me?"

"Just be careful, not like your professor."

"How about Sheriff Chaney? Why do you suppose he framed Gatini? There must have been a more likely candidate."

"I guess they needed someone who was here in them days, and who knew Scott. Look, I don't figure it was Chaney who conned the thing up. The brains of the sheriff's department belong to Josh Kirk, though he wouldn't have been around the summer Scott was killed neither. I can tell you, though, one of them bastards ain't no better than the other, but everyone says it was Kirk who thought up arresting Alberto."

"What do you think of Smithers, the ex-state cop?"

"Ain't never been face-to-face with him, and I hope it stays that way."

"For your sake, I hope it stays that way, too," I said as he rode off through the trees.

The air was cooling and the sky was graying toward black when I reached the trail that led down to town. Retracing the way I'd come that morning, I realized the roads weren't a meaningless meander. Like an ancient streambed, they followed the path of least resistance, sticking to the mountain's contours and flowing around sharp rock outcroppings. I hoped my attempts to find a killer—or *killers*—weren't a meaningless meander, either.

I stopped on the hill above the stable and again looked out over Blind Spring. Now, its lights glittered, and I could make out its well-defined limits and the vehicles driving its streets.

It seemed as if a shadow was crossing over me.

Lifting my head, I saw a huge bird outlined against the star-splattered sky. At first, I thought it might be an owl, but I quickly realized it wasn't. The black shape swooped down over the top of McGraw's stable, then, like a warplane, zoomed high again. Whether it was a soaring eagle or a vengeful hawk, I couldn't tell.

For some reason, a line from the ballad book surfaced in my head.

And where hae you been, my handsome young man?

Not so damn handsome.

Not so damn sure.

Goddamn Grant and those ballads.

18

Saturday night might have been the whiskey man's big one, the night the movie theater was jammed full, the night the miners and timbermen could cut free and whoop it up, but you'd never have known it from the deserted street in front of the hotel. The hellraisers must have been smart enough to stay in their own neighborhoods.

From *New Jersey*'s balcony, the only apparent action was an occasional sheriff's patrol passing by. Below me, I could see the boots and shins of the mine guard on the front porch. He was a nighttime guard, never there in the daylight. When I'd come down from the mountains, he was settled into the same chair where he'd been the night Grant and I had come back from our long walk. He'd shot me a stare, but said nothing.

Even the alley beside the Briggs Hotel was empty. The black car and its driver were nowhere to be seen. Over the private entrance, a bare bulb threw a circle of light on the ground where the automobile was usually parked.

At one point, a car stopped in front of the place and the deputy left his post on the porch and stepped down to meet it. Through the vehicle's open window, the cop talked to someone, and I wondered who it might be. Fred Chaney? Josh Kirk? Smithers? There was no way to know.

Eventually, looking no more enlightened than before, the deputy returned to his seat, and the car drove off, maybe on its way to break up John Summerset's bootleg sales, or maybe just to keep up the search for the union organizer.

I wondered what Stephen O'Dell was doing. Was he holed up in a company house, preaching his message to a group of Briggs' miners? Again, I wondered whether I should have turned down his offer to work together. As had been the case with the sheriff's car, there was no way to know, and I tried to shake off my confusion.

Keep working, the boss had ordered.

Sure. I guessed I'd broken that commandment already. After taking the horse back to the stable, I'd returned to the hotel rather than going to the Blind Spring Bakery to follow up the whiskey man's lead. I'd been tired, and I didn't see how the bakers were going to help me much. As it was, Ben McGraw had been full of questions. Again, I'd tried to get away without answering them, but not before he'd asked one that jarred me.

"Are you planning to stay in town and see this thing through?"

How do you answer a question like that? Why had he even asked it?

"Yeah. I'm planning to see this thing through," I'd told him. Then I'd walked away rather than stand around and chat. Poor form, maybe, but I hoped he'd understand my mind wasn't set for more talk.

I had the feeling that I'd only begun my shift in the mines, had only just climbed aboard the cart that would roll me down through the underground passages, where I might get lost, where the supports might collapse and the black rock come tumbling in on me.

For the time being, I was content to lean against the white column at the corner of the balcony. I wasn't conscious that my mind was playing tricks on me until I felt the dizziness in my head. It was almost like I was floating away, out into the night, until I was hovering above the streetlights and staring back at myself staring out. If I'd had my wits about me, I'd have bought some of Summerset's whiskey and drunk myself to sleep.

I was watching a truck's headlights shoot up Briggs Boulevard when I heard the skirmish upstairs. It began with loud talk, and then the words seemed to boil and spill over. A piece of furniture fell. Or was thrown. Soon a man was yelling full-throat.

I leaned over the railing and looked up toward the *District of Columbia,* but there was nothing to see except a haze of light.

Below me, I could see the deputy's boots. He hadn't budged. Could be he'd heard such scenes before and didn't want to get involved. Could be he knew enough to stay out of Briggs business, whatever that business was.

Upstairs, the angry man demanded, "How could you do something like that?"

A woman answered in a calmer voice, in words I couldn't make out. Again, there was the cracking sound of furniture, or something hard, hitting the floor. Then she screamed.

I couldn't tell if she was mad or afraid, but I suddenly felt like I had to find out.

"You goddamn lying bitch! You mislead me over and over!" the man bawled.

Stretching over the railing, I checked on the mine guard again. He was still blissfully ignoring the ruckus.

I grabbed the column before I knew what I was doing and stepped up on the rail. After twisting myself around, I was able to glimpse the fourth-story balcony, though my eyes were only at floor level. The room's door was ajar and a window was propped open.

"I should have known I couldn't trust you!" the man yelled.

"You're crazy! You always were crazy!" she yelled back. "Why must you always set up these scenes?"

Their words were clearer, but I still couldn't see anything.

"I didn't set up anything, you goddamn cunt! I can't stand you anymore!" he shouted.

"I could never stand you," she replied. "I wish we'd never met!"

There was another crack of wood against wood, and then someone was pounding at the hall door, calling for the man and woman to open up.

"Go away, you bastards!" he bellowed.

I took the opportunity to hoist myself up until I was balanced on the outer lip of the balcony. Inside the room, Briggs Junior was waving his arms like a lunatic.

"I'll run you out of this goddamn town!" he yelled at the woman.

"Miss Bascomb," the lady in the dress shop had called her. Now, she was naked except for a necklace and black high-heeled shoes.

There was more pounding at the front door. For an instant, I thought she was going to open it. Jim Briggs must have thought so, too.

"Don't move, you whore!" he screamed, jumping up on the bed so violently that the springs groaned and the frame shook. Then, to whoever was outside the door, "I told you to go away!"

Miss Bascomb backed away from the door and seemed to be edging toward the bathroom for cover. But her eyes stayed on Junior. She wasn't one to cower.

Briggs whirled around on the bed and pounded the mattress. He was wearing a pink negligée that was so sheer you could see his muscles contort as he thrashed about. He shook his fist at her. Then his hand reached out for a heavy glass ashtray on a table next to the bed. He hefted it and hurled it at her with more curses.

Miss Bascomb froze when the ashtray crashed against the bathroom door and glared at him. With her hand resting on the swell of her hip, she stood her ground, challenging him.

The hall door rattled from the pounding.

"I don't ever want you here again!" screamed Junior.

"Easily done," she said flatly.

He picked up a whiskey bottle and hopped off the bed. As he staggered across the room at her, I decided I couldn't take it any longer, and leaped over the railing and ran into the bedroom.

Briggs didn't seem to have any idea I was there, but Miss Bascomb saw me. At least, her eyes moved in my direction.

I reached for his shoulders and missed, but managed to grab the back of the negligée and pulled him backward with all my strength. The sheer material ripped, but not before he'd tumbled to the floor. He'd been so drunkenly off-balance that decking him was simpler than I'd imagined.

I was about to kick him in the head if I had to, when Dr. Anders Corman and a deputy sheriff came through the balcony door. Without asking what I was doing, they rushed around me and lifted young Briggs onto the bed. Corman had his medical bag with him, and soon the deputy was holding Jim Briggs down and the doctor was opening his black satchel.

My eyes went to Miss Bascomb. For a second, I couldn't help but admire her body. She couldn't have been any older than I was, and might have still been in her teens. She was leaning her bare back against a cabinet, watching the doctor work on Briggs' son. When she realized I was staring at her, she cupped her hands in front of her dark pubic hair and slowly made her way to the bathroom, slamming the door behind her.

Before long, Corman was shutting his black bag. "That'll take care of the ruffian."

"What'd you give him?" I asked.

"Nothing that won't wear off by morning. He'll wake up with a hell of a hangover, which is a lot less than he deserves. He may not even remember what happened."

I hoped he wouldn't. I didn't want Jim Briggs to vent his belligerence on me the next time I saw him. On the other hand, I hoped Miss Bascomb *would* remember me.

After a few minutes, Briggs stopped ratting around and relaxed. The pink negligée was balled up around his shoulders. When he was barely squirming, the doctor looked at the deputy. "Spectacle's over," he said. "You can go now."

"He is a spectacle," I said, as soon as the cop was gone. "He could never run for politics on the Prohibition ticket."

"Or on a church-and-home platform," said Corman. "He's a terrible hedonist. I don't know how you ended up in this room, but I'm glad you did. All we need is for this brat to beat up his girlfriend."

"I was out on my balcony and heard the squabble. At first, I tried to ignore it, but, when I heard the girl scream, I climbed up."

"You did the right thing. Don't worry about barging in—you won't land in any trouble. He could have really hurt the girl. Even Timothy's fed up with the boy. There's been too much trouble too many times."

"Is he crazy, like she said?"

"I suppose that could be an explanation, though I'm not sure how Dr. Freud would diagnose him. I'm no great believer in this new psychology, you understand. If you'd ask him when he was lucid, Jim Briggs might say he's caught a fever in the mountains. He'll always blame it on Blind Spring. Some men get jungle fever; he's got mountain fever. Of course, the truth is nothing like that. God knows the things he's done to that girl, but he wasn't any better back in Philadelphia. That's why his father brought him here. Timothy was hoping isolation and hard work would do Junior good."

Pointing to the bathroom door, I asked, "She's his girlfriend, then?"

"You could put it like that. At least it would be nicer than the truth."

"So, what'll happen to him now?"

"I'll try to talk his father into sending him away. No one needs his aggravation, considering the union organizer and moonshiners and all the other problems we've got right now."

"I take it he's not crucial to the mine's management."

Corman laughed. "Look at him. How could he be 'crucial' to anything? He's a playboy, pure and simple. He likes the money from his father's enterprise, but he doesn't have the spunk to run anything himself. Timothy had hoped James would straighten up. Now and then, the boy will make a show of being interested in some aspect of the business. He'll dive into a flurry of activity, but a week later he'll go on a binge. He's not so unique in that regard. You know what they say about the children of successful fathers."

"It all must be very frustrating for Mr. Briggs."

"To all of us. Sooner or later, Timothy will need a young man with more brains than Fred Chaney to help him. He was serious yesterday when he said he could use someone like you. He mentioned you again later. He reads people rapidly. Like all money men, he acts on impulse some times. You could do far worse than to work for Timothy. It would be a more secure life than this . . . this folkloring."

We stood in awkward silence for a minute. Then I took another look at the closed bathroom door and said, "If you don't need me, I'll be going back to my room."

"Consider Timothy's employment offer," said Corman.

"It may have been your destiny that brought you to Blind Spring."

Destiny, hell.

I went out the door, down the hall, past the deputy at the top of the staircase.

Why was I so damn valuable to everyone in Blind Spring? First Stephen O'Dell had wanted me on his side to help blow Briggs' ship out of the water. Now Timothy Briggs wanted me on that same ship to add more ballast.

I never was good at puzzles.

19

Sunday morning, shaving, I almost didn't recognize my face in the mirror. My skin had picked up some color from being out and around, had reddened on its way to summer tan. More than that, though, I thought I looked older. The expression on my face no longer seemed to belong to the college boy of six months before. Was that the result of too many nights spent with a gun beside my pillow? Was that what being a detective was really all about?

Carefully, I freed my mustache from the stubble imprisoning it. Once I'd razored away the soapy lather, I could see the mustache was nearly full. For whatever good it was. It still didn't make me a movie hero, and D. W. Griffith still wasn't standing in line to offer me a part in one of his pictures.

Keep working.

Christ.

The evening before, after I'd returned from Suze Chester's, I'd wanted there to be a new message waiting for me, a new telegram from New York. I'd wanted some words that would translate into HELP ON THE WAY.

No such luck. Didn't the boss realize I was a rookie in a

strange town where there were more cops, more mine guards, per square inch than there were politicians in Washington?

I guessed he didn't. In fact, he probably didn't even know Frank Grant hadn't told me who we were working for. Imagine how dumb I'd sound if I wired a question like that!

Again, Sunday morning as I passed through the lobby, there was no telegram awaiting me at the desk. What there was, however, was a small envelope addressed to me in a neat script. I knew from the expensive paper that it wasn't another Pompey Smash note.

I took the thing back to the dining room and, after I'd ordered breakfast, tore open the ivory wrapper.

> *Thank you for coming to my rescue last night. I hope you will pay me a visit at my home at 117 Dutters Drive this afternoon. I will be free all day on Sunday.*
> *Clair Bascomb*

There was a P.S. with a telephone number if I couldn't make it. Fat chance I was going to make such a call. I guess I'd known from the second I saw her climb out of the Ford on Thursday afternoon that I'd meet her if I could. I'd even tricked her address out of the woman in the dress shop.

Anyone who watched me eat breakfast that morning might have believed I was absorbed in the act. Anyone who saw me later on the hotel's front porch might have believed I was deep in studying the newspaper I'd bought. Anyone who believed such stuff was easily deceived. What was really on my mind was Miss Bascomb—*Clair*. I admit it now, I admitted it then.

Adventure and women, that's what I'd hoped being a detective would be all about, not sleeping with one eye open, gun in hand. The visit to the Blind Spring Bakery and everything else would simply have to wait, I told myself. Going to Miss

Bascomb's was part of my job. She'd surely know a lot about Briggs Junior, and maybe about his old man and the behind-the-scenes scuttlebutt in the *District of Columbia*. She'd have a way of seeing them that I hadn't tapped into yet. She'd have information I couldn't pick up anywhere else.

Still, there was a lot to wonder about her. Cool and defiant under Junior's fire. Naked, obviously convinced she'd done nothing wrong.

And what of Jim Briggs? With his violent temper, was he a bigger player in Blind Spring intrigues than Dr. Corman had let on? Hell, it was tough to picture him tracking down Grant in the middle of the night, or, five years earlier, hiking into the woods to slaughter a prospector. But you never could tell.

A church bell rang. Down the block, a couple crossed Briggs Boulevard. Tagging along behind them was a little boy holding the hand of his older sister. They were all dressed for Sunday morning. Once, I too had marched to church like that, scrubbed and polished and wearing my best.

You never know where the choices you make will take you. You never know how you'll end up. There were times I felt like I should have never left the university.

Anyway, I had a couple hours to kill before I could show up at Miss Bascomb's door. I opened the newspaper, praying it would tell me more about Grant's death than the little that Sheriff Chaney had on Friday. But Grant's corpse in the coal car wasn't played up big in the Charleston paper. There'd been no headlines on Saturday, either. It was almost like there'd been no murder, or else it just wasn't something out of the ordinary, something newsworthy.

The big story again concerned Warren Harding. He was to deliver a national radio address from St. Louis, a feat that no president had ever performed before. Harding, who'd given a batch of rear-platform speeches since embarking on his "Voyage of Understanding," was acting his role in the grand new age of communications, reported the newspaper. Transatlantic radio messages were possible now between New York and London.

If so, why was I so damn isolated from the detective agency? Why was it harder to communicate with Blind Spring, West Virginia, than with Paris or London?

Hell, I sounded like Jim Briggs. It was as if I'd been infected with the black plague of doubt, which had to be every bit as dangerous as the influenza epidemic that had run wild at the end of the war.

I had to get going again, had to get cured.

The sun was aiming for afternoon high when I spotted the boy with the Bible passing the porch.

"I'm new in town," I said to him. "Can you tell me where Dutters Drive is?"

Luckily, he could.

20

Dutters Drive was a twenty-minute roundabout walk up the steep residential hillside. Hers was the only house I saw on the tree-lined street. I couldn't have been wrong. The numbers were clear—117. I stopped for a second to try to figure out how the bright yellow structure came by its address. Could have been Timothy Briggs's sense of whimsy again, or else someone was leaving numbers for future suburban expansion.

The place was two stories tall, with bay windows and loads of brown curlicued trim. The roofline consisted of several levels of snowbreaking slant, like the carpenters had gone berserk. It looked more like a big dollhouse than anything else. The only elements of realism, the only blemishes, were the power and phone lines overhanging the well-tended flower garden and attaching to the house's right side.

I stood outside the gate a while, staring at the building, telling myself it was surely one place Grant hadn't visited on Thursday. Then I went up the brick walk to the front door.

She must have been watching me from a window, because she opened the door before I even knocked.

"I'm Bill Edmonson," I said. "I got your note this morning."

"Clair Bascomb." She opened the door wider.

Strange, these awkward introductions with a woman I'd already seen naked. Or had Saturday night's scene only made things more awkward?

"You look awfully hot. It's cooler inside. The trees shade the house nicely," she said as she led me down a short hallway. If she felt any awkwardness, she sure didn't show it.

She was wearing a short peach-colored dress, almost like a tunic but belted in with a strip of material below her hips, and it showed off her legs in their sheer flesh-tinted stockings to fine effect.

She led me into a room as bright as any I'd ever seen. The walls were bright red and lace curtains framed the windows, allowing in as much sunlight as possible and making the plush red sofa and chairs shine even brighter.

She must have been watching me soak it in. "What do you think?" she asked, as if she was proud of it.

"Pretty classy. Not exactly what I expected."

"What *did* you expect?"

I laughed, the awkwardness vanishing. "I don't know. It's not like other rooms I've seen in town."

"That's the idea. Sit down. Would you like something to drink—some wine or some tea?"

"Some tea would be nice," I said, deciding to stay away from liquor while I was working.

"I'll be right back." She went through open sliding doors into an adjoining dining room. Her high heels gave her a lilt as she moved. Her dress swayed from her narrow shoulders. She disappeared into yet another room, probably the kitchen, and I sank into the red sofa, feeling like I'd fallen into a dream world. No coal camp grit and grime at Clair Bascomb's.

In front of the couch was a long low coffee table. Like the arms of the sofa and chairs, like every other surface in the red room, the coffee table was covered with a lacy doily. The doilies, the lace curtains—at least my mother would have found something to approve of. "Dollhouse" wasn't a bad description at all.

On top of the coffee table was a metal stereoscope and a box of stereoptic slides. Like the frilly doily beneath them, I found the stereoscope and slides to be odd touches for a modern girl. In most homes, such old-fashioned paraphernalia had been relegated to the attic with the advent of movies and Victrolas. Still, in one corner, Clair Bascomb had a modern phonograph.

I reached over and, without studying it, slid the top slide into the stereoscope. Lifting the eyepieces to my face, I moved the slide toward my eyes until it came in focus and the scene popped into three dimensions. It only took me a second to realize it wasn't like the slides of European cathedrals and Egyptian pyramids that we used to have at home.

In an elaborate drawing room, filled with potted palms, a buxom lady was bent over a carved-legged table. Her white bloomers had been ripped open at the rear, exposing her buttocks. Next to her was a man with a black handlebar mustache. He was holding a whip. It must have been Jim Briggs' favorite slide.

"There are others, possibly more to your fancy, whatever your fancy is," said Miss Bascomb, returning to the room, a silver serving tray in her hands.

Whatever your fancy is.

"I'm not much interested in stereoptic slides," I said.

"What *are* you interested in?" Her knees together, she bent down, almost in a curtsy, and put the tray on the coffee table in front of me. In addition to a silver tea set and china cups, there were cheese, crackers, and cookies—another "high tea."

"I suppose I want to be certain you're alright," I said. "Briggs didn't hurt you last night, did he?"

She shook her head. "I don't know if *Junior* would honestly hurt me, but I'm glad you saved me from finding out."

There was a bite of sarcasm in the way she pronounced *Junior*.

In her shoes, I'd probably have been sarcastic about the bastard, too.

"Cream or sugar?" she asked as she sat down next to me.

"A tad of sugar, Miss Bascomb."

"Call me Clair. I certainly intend to call you Bill." When she wasn't screaming at Jim Briggs, she had a soft voice that I couldn't quite place geographically. "What was it Dr. Corman told me last night after you'd left Junior's room? You're a college professor, or is it a student?"

"I'm an assistant to Professor Frank Grant. At least, I was until he was killed. We came to Blind Spring to gather folklore."

"Men come to town for all sorts of reasons," she said, handing me the cup of tea. "Dr. Corman didn't tell me much. I asked him who you were so I could invite you here to thank you."

"How long have you been in Blind Spring?"

"This fall, I'll have been here two years. I came in October 1921."

"How did you end up here? It doesn't seem like the kind of place you'd pick out of the atlas."

"How did you end up here?" she asked back.

I sipped at the hot tea. "I told you. I came with Professor Grant."

"Why didn't you leave after the professor was killed?"

"I'm in no rush. I'm being paid to find old songs and stories. I'd like to wait around and see what the police learn about his death. Grant's family will want to know," I lied. I didn't know if Grant had a family or not.

"I imagine they will, but I don't like to talk of murders and all. I try to banish such topics from my house. My visitors prefer it that way."

"It's hard sometimes to keep the outside world out."

Her green eyes settled on mine. "You can try."

A telephone rang in another room. Clair smoothed her peach-colored dress and went to answer it. When she was gone,

I put down my teacup and walked around. The red walls were loaded with photographs and paintings. The one that caught my eye wasn't a Rubens nude or one of the geisha scenes. It was of Clair.

She was lying on a sofa, the very sofa in the red room, and she was wearing only a short black chemise. The photographer had been standing at her feet, aiming up the length of her reclining body. The chemise was hiked to her waist, and her long legs were bent at the knees, up in the air, apart, inviting the camera between them.

"A portrait by a friend," she said, having returned so quietly I hadn't heard her.

"Not Jim Briggs, I hope."

"God, no. Junior isn't *smart* enough to figure out how to work a camera. In fact, he doesn't know how to do much of anything. He can pick up a phone, though. The call was from him."

"Was he apologizing for last night?"

"He wanted me to come to the hotel for dinner this evening. I imagine Dr. Corman has told the old man about it, and Junior's been tongue-lashed into submission. He said he'll be leaving tomorrow, and tonight will be my last chance to see him for some time."

"I'll go, so you can get ready."

"Oh, I won't be going to the hotel. I wouldn't even consider it. I'm not insane enough to voluntarily be in the same room with him so soon. Maybe never again. I told him I was busy."

"I don't want to get you crossed with the big man's son."

"How could I be more crossed with him? Besides, he's the one leaving town, not me. Even his father knows Junior's worthless."

"You know Timothy Briggs, then?"

She sat back down on the sofa and crossed those long legs. "Actually, I've never met Mr. Briggs. He doesn't get out of his room very often. He runs this town from his bed." She let out a laugh that was almost a giggle. "He's never invited me into his bed. He's probably too old, or thinks he is. But I've seen more than enough of his son to last a lifetime."

"So you don't think the old man's going to blame his son's indiscretions on you?"

"Indiscretions?" She laughed again, this time a deeper laugh from her throat. "You're funny. You're so young."

"No younger than you. Maybe older," I said, deciding she must have been in her teens when she first came to Blind Spring.

"In some ways, I'm much older than you. I went straight into life, with no college."

Christ, she sounded just like Grant jabbing at me. I tried my question again. "So Timothy Briggs isn't going to throw you out of town?"

"He'd have a tough time trying," she said with assurance. "No, he abides me. I know too much about Junior, and, anyway, I'm useful to him."

"You said you'd never met him."

"Not face-to-face, but he still knows about me. I've met many of his associates. When the railroad biggies come to town, or Briggs' friends from Philadelphia, there's not much for them to do here. I know they say 'nice girls don't,' but if all girls didn't, there'd be a multitude of frustrated men. I'm not a tease, Bill Edmonson. I'm not one of those prim-and-proper ladies who used to put on low-cut gowns, or strapped bustles on behind, and then acted like Queen Victoria. I know what I'm doing, and so did they, I hope. I'm not embarrassed about it. The old man himself has sent his business associates to me, and I send them back to him in a better mood. I do quite well here. I'm not one of the nickel-and-dime chippies that you find elsewhere in this town."

Looking around the room, at its furnishings, at the art gallery on the wall, it was easy to see she did quite well and that no one would accuse her of being a nickel-and-dime chippie.

"Then you must know all the investors who Briggs wines and dines," I said.

"I don't tell tales out of school, Bill. You'll learn to appreciate my discretion. And, besides, there are men who I'll have nothing to do with. For instance, no one could pay me enough to put up with Fred Chaney."

"The sheriff?" McGraw had said Chaney was a whoremonger.

The curls of her short brown hair shook when she nodded.

"You mean he's worse than Junior?" I asked.

"He's worse . . . and not as rich."

I remembered Thursday night. Clair had left the hotel just after Chaney had entered it. But I had no way of knowing whether there was a connection between his coming and her going.

"He's that bad, huh?"

"That bad," she answered, glancing away from me and out the window like she was bored.

"Where are you from?" I asked, trying to get her started again.

"You mean originally?"

"Yes."

"I was . . . You want to know too much. I'm not a piece of folklore. I don't know any old songs, only the new ones."

Her skirt swirled as she jumped up from the sofa and crossed the room to the Victrola. For a moment, she seemed to be thinking, then she put on a recording and lowered the needle onto the grooves.

"What's this? I don't know this song," I said as the jazzy horns blared from the speaker.

"It's called 'Lonesome Mama Blues.' You can dance, can't you?"

"Passably."

"Then, I'll teach you to dance better. You'll have something to show for your afternoon," she said, reaching out a hand to me.

It was weird to be dancing with her in the bright room in the middle of a Sunday afternoon. She played recording after recording, and sometimes we moved around fast to the beat, building up a sweat on the June day, and sometimes we pressed together slow, barely budging.

Then we were clasping each other, not holding each other neatly like waltzers, but grasping, like there was no one else in the world but her and me. My hands were sliding down her back to her hips, then raising her skirt and rubbing at the flesh of her thighs.

A lightness came into my head, like the uncertain giddiness that comes when you're riding a ferris wheel, swinging up higher all the time, toward the soft sky, and when it gets to the top of its loop, and you're far above the ground, the wheel stops, leaving you stranded at the heights for a long breath in a cart waving in the wind like Old Glory, unable to distinguish between your feelings and your surroundings, and then the wheel begins to circle again, and the cart is dropping toward the earth.

"Let's go to bed," she said.

21

I imagined her sticky dampness still on me when I awoke on Monday morning. I could still feel her legs around me, could still feel the swell of her breasts, their diamond-hard nipples. My prick hardened again at the memory of her.

I reached across the bed, but she was gone.

Dull awakening. I still felt groggy from the night, from the wine she'd brought upstairs after we'd made love the first time. How had the hours disappeared? No time on a ferris wheel. Sunday had melted away.

I heard water running in the bathtub.

When she came into the bedroom, I was propped up on her pillows, the cool smooth sheets pulled to my waist. I could smell her powdered skin.

"Morning."

"Morning."

She was wearing a thin gown over her underclothes. She opened her wardrobe and searched for the proper dress. When she'd decided on one, she carefully spread it over the back of a chair. Then she sat on a stool in front of a huge round mirror.

I watched as she began to draw a brush across her eyes, drawing in such a way that, in the mirror's reflection, their green became emerald. She was fine-boned, and so slim-waisted that there was a deep indentation at the base of her spine where her buttocks flared out, high and tight. It was easy to see why her friends and admirers wanted to photograph her, to put her on film, easy to see why they bought her things. The lady in the dress shop had known, hadn't she? After she'd given me Miss Bascomb's address, she'd asked if I wanted a gift for my lady friend.

Clair angled her head to check her left eye. "Did you ever notice how we never see ourselves exactly right in mirrors? We never see ourselves precisely as others do. It's always in reverse. It's a lie. It's never right side left."

"I never thought about it," I said.

She stopped applying her eye makeup and seemed to glance at my reflection in front of her. "You wouldn't. Men wouldn't. You probably believe all this attention to powder and paint is silly and unnecessary, but you admire it all the same. Being admired is important to my livelihood."

"I guess it is."

"Of course it is." She picked up a lipstick. "No one would pay me what I'm worth if I dressed like a miner's wife."

I wondered whether Kayce Powell's wife would trade in her company house and baby to swap places with Clair. Somehow, I doubted it.

She looked at her lips in the mirror, then put down the lipstick and screwed on a pair of earrings. Next, she opened a drawer in the vanity and pulled out a pair of black stockings. Her gown fell open when she lifted her leg and began sliding the first one on. It was as if she was inviting again, like her pose in the photo on the wall downstairs. First her foot, then her ankle, her calf, her knee disappeared inside the black sheath. When the silk had covered part of her thigh, she affixed a garter.

She pulled the other stocking onto her foot and up over her ankle—those ankles that had hooked about my waist—and the dark sheath slid smoothly, delicately, toward her knee—those knees that had held my sides—and then she extended her trim leg and pulled until the stocking top was at her thigh and her pale leg had become a luminous black.

I wanted to pull her into the bed, strip the clothes off her piece by soft piece, and begin Sunday afternoon again.

She knew I was studying her and, from the smile on her lips, was enjoying it. She leaned over and slid her feet into a pair of shoes on the floor next to the dressing table. They were black and conservative, not the modern high heels I'd only seen her wearing. Then she stood and turned so she could view herself in the mirror, from front, back, and every other angle. At one point, she reached down to adjust her stockings more to her liking.

Finally, after seeming to get lost in her own reflection for a second, she faced me and announced, "The show's over."

"Too bad," I said.

"You're going to have to go." She pointed to my stuff, which was piled on a chair near the bed.

Feeling a little hurt, I tossed off the sheets and grabbed my shirt. I dressed in a rush. There's no sexy elegance about a man dressing, not about me dressing, anyway. She paid me no mind, not even when I strapped on the holster.

Sunday, I'd been nervous about what she'd say when I took off my coat and unveiled the gun. She must have felt it as we danced, and I'd feared she'd accuse me of bringing the mean world into her salon. But she'd said nothing, hadn't even stared at me cockeyed. Those eyes, I supposed, were never cockeyed, never less than perfect and cool. Maybe I was wrong, but I'd somehow gotten the idea she had other visitors who packed pistols, that, to her, they were something men had to strap on, just as there were things women must.

I put on my suitcoat and, when I turned back to her, she was a completely changed woman. A dark conservative dress that matched the shoes she'd selected covered all her straps and underwear. She could have been a schoolteacher.

"Going to a funeral?" I asked.

She smiled. "For your information, one of my clients likes me to dress this way. He prefers me to appear proper and severe—on the outside, at least."

"What about underneath?"

"Everything's different beneath the surface, isn't it? He's an odd duck. He has his own private railway car and, whenever he travels through here, he stops for me and we take a little ride."

"Must be nice. First-class, huh?"

"Always, if I have anything to say about it."

"Did you ever consider riding away from here and doing something else?"

"What else would I possibly do? Work in a textile mill? Sell flowers? Be a secretary? I don't like to be poor, and I always repay my debts."

She looked straight at me and I got the message that she'd invited me to her house, her room, to repay me for Saturday night, clear and simple, fee in hand.

"What will you be doing today?" she asked. "Will you go searching for some old fiddle player in the hills?"

"You never know. I just might."

"You know where I live now," she said. "Call me, if you want to come back. Not for free, of course, but I wouldn't mind seeing you again. I don't see many nice young men my own age."

"I thought you were decades older than me, and so much more mature."

She laughed. "Stop it." Her laugh reminded me of the earlier, softer Clair, and I could tell she expected I'd return.

Did she also know she'd been my first lover? Probably. She was the kind of girl who could sense such things.

She was staring into her mirror, stealing another glimpse at her face and body to be sure she was made up just right, when I left her.

Outside on Dutters Drive, the day felt fiery already as I walked back to the Briggs Hotel.

22

"Where you been, boy?" called Sheriff Fred Chaney as I started up the hotel steps. His fat head was poking halfway out the passenger window of a car that had screeched to a stop in front of the place.

"Seeing the sights," I answered as calmly as I could.

"That shouldn't take you long around here," he said. "We been looking for you. I sent Smithers to find you last night, and again this morning. You found somewhere else to sleep?"

"I told you Friday that I was going to continue our work."

"And I told you, you'd be wisest to go home. You folklorers lack good sense, or is it a family problem?"

"Maybe both," I said, smiling, trying to slide out of an argument.

"Well, the least you can do is get the professor's damn trunk out of my office. It's taking up space. Another day, and I might charge you ground rent. I thought you'd arranged to take care of it."

Christ. You mean the detective agency hadn't? I'd just assumed they had.

Keep working.

"I thought it was taken care of," I said.

"I hear they sent the body home from Wild Stream, but no one's done nothing about the trunk."

"I'll come over to the office later."

"Tend to it now," insisted Chaney. He motioned to the back door of the black car. "Climb in. We'll be heading back that way in a couple minutes."

Short of a needless commotion, there wasn't much I could do. So, I opened the door and crawled in, knowing full well that the side trip would throw off my plans a little. I'd wanted to take a bath and then look up the Italian bakers that the whiskey man had told me about. So I'd lose an hour or two, so what?

Deputy Smithers was driving, and once I'd gotten in, he inched forward a few yards and turned into the alley beside the hotel.

"Going up to see Mr. Briggs?" I asked Chaney.

"Not hardly. Just playing taxi," he said.

After the car was parked by the private entrance, Smithers opened the door, stretched his big frame out, and went through the door and, I guessed, up the elevator to the *District of Columbia*.

Chaney drummed his fingers on the dashboard, then twisted around to face me. "I heard about your big heroics on Saturday night."

"Yeah?"

"Yeah. You should have let Junior do whatever he wanted to do to the whore. They're made for each other."

Whatever had happened when Chaney had visited Clair Bascomb, they obviously hated each other equally. You couldn't pay her enough to put up with him, and he thought she deserved anything she got. Staring at his pale bloated face, I had to side with Clair.

"The boy's an ass," huffed Chaney. "I don't know where he gets his blood. He ain't like his old man at all. Junior don't know coal from shale, and he's jealous of anyone gets along with his father."

"You think he's jealous of you?" I asked.

"Sure he is, and I never did nothing to him, though I'd like to give him a good whupping."

At least they all agreed about one thing. Clair, Chaney, Dr. Corman, none of them had any use for Junior. Thinking back to Friday afternoon, it was easy to believe Timothy Briggs didn't have much use for him, either.

"You heard any more details about what happened to Professor Grant?" I asked, trying to pry some info out of him. "What'd they learn at the autopsy?"

"Nothing new, far as I know. We just suppose your Grant was roaming at night somewhere he shouldn't have been, and he stumbled into a coal car. It was an accident, I'd say, but it should be a lesson to roamers."

"Hard to accidentally stumble into a coal car."

"Hard, but ain't unheard of. You been warned about the things going on in town. I kind of like you, boy. I don't want to see you end the same way."

The door to the hotel opened. Smithers stepped out lugging a small trunk. After he walked to the rear of the car to get rid of it, he climbed back into the driver's seat but didn't drive away.

"Where is the bastard?" grumbled Chaney.

"He said he's coming," answered Smithers.

A moment later, the private door opened again and out came Jim Briggs, a suitcase in his hand. Junior moved to the car and opened the passenger door without looking. He seemed surprised when he saw me.

"New deputy, Fred?" he said.

"Boy needed a ride, that's all."

"You always were a helpful chap," said Junior sarcastically.

"Your father thinks so."

"My father's senile. Between you and Anders Corman, he doesn't get any better."

"I ain't no Corman lover," said Chaney. "But you brought this on yourself. It was your antics the other night, and you know it. Corman ain't got much to do with it, other than telling your father what you done. Mr. Briggs has been warning you."

Junior didn't bother to respond. I slid across the seat to make room for him, and he put his suitcase between us, as if to mark his territory. Sitting there like that, I couldn't help wondering how much he recalled about Saturday night, about me pulling him to the floor.

At first, Briggs and Chaney stared out their windows as Smithers sped through the nearly-empty Monday-morning streets. I was glad we went to the train station first, because it gave me a chance to pick up a little more of the tension between them. I decided that if Stephen O'Dell could have witnessed it, he'd have thought it hilarious. That's if the union organizer had a sense of humor. At any rate, it would have changed how he saw the people he was fighting.

I mean, here was Chaney, the high sheriff, being nicer to me than to Briggs Junior. And the son, for his part, was jealous of the sway the sheriff and the doctor had over his father. And neither of the two was a Corman lover. Meanwhile, the son was apparently being shipped out of town, at Dr. Corman's insistence, and the son's girlfriend was tired of Junior's ways, unreverent about the old man, and downright spiteful about the sheriff.

The way they were at each other's throats was enough to make me laugh, though I didn't like calling Clair "the son's girlfriend." Once I might have described her so, but now I knew her. Still, it was better than calling her "the whore," as Chaney had.

I decided that if O'Dell had known the half of it, he'd have played one off against the other. *Divide and conquer.* It wasn't a bad philosophy for me, either.

At the station, I got out of the car with them. There were more sparks when Junior realized Chaney had luggage, too.

"You being sent to Philly to keep tabs on me?" Briggs asked. "That's out of your jurisdiction, isn't it?"

"I'll be going part way with you," answered Chaney.

"Shit, it's bad enough to be deported by my old man, without having the law escort me to the state line. That son of a bitch Corman must have set my father against me a hundred percent."

"I'm not exactly along to breathe down your neck," said Chaney.

"What do you call it, then?" challenged Junior.

"I was on my way out of town last week when Mr. Briggs called me back," explained Chaney. "You remember? I was taking the wop to the pen, and then I was going to Charleston. But your father was so damn worried about the union organizer that I came back. Now the heat's off, and I'm going to Wheeling for a little vacation. I've earned it."

"Have a thrilling time," said Briggs, lighting a cigarette as he hurried toward the train.

"So, you're not concerned about the union organizer any longer?" I asked Chaney.

He stared at me like he couldn't believe my question. "I'd say that one's pretty much history. Blind Spring's sealed up tight again, or I wouldn't leave. Josh Kirk can damn well take care of any little kindling flares up. Now, you get over to the office and take care of that trunk."

I watched him swagger across the station platform. As before—as always—the platform was lined with deputy sheriffs questioning people. When I turned away, Deputy Smithers was hollering at someone and the Murry County Customs Bureau was in full swing.

23

Chief Deputy Josh Kirk was leaned back in Fred Chaney's chair, his feet propped up on the desk. He smoked a cigar and talked on the phone, playing sheriff to the hilt. Maybe he was getting his orders from the *District of Columbia* for the day. The office air was stale from his cigar smoke.

"Got to go," he told the person at the other end "Train just hit town, and someone's come in."

As he stretched forward to hang up the telephone, I said, "Sheriff Chaney asked me to see about Professor Grant's trunk. Apparently, it's still here."

"It's still here alright," said Kirk, swinging his feet off the desk. He was a lot more limber than Chaney. He still had to work for a living.

He walked across the office, found the right key on the ring attached to his gunbelt, and unlocked the munitions room door.

"There it is. We're getting in new supplies and need the space. We thought you'd taken care of it," he said.

"So did I."

Kirk bent down and moved a carton of shells from the top of the trunk, and we each grabbed an end and carried it out to the main office. I undid the latches and peeked inside while he locked up the armory.

"It's all there," he said. "No safer place in Blind Spring. Tell you what, you give me the address and I'll have a couple of my men drag the thing over to the station for you."

I ran my choices through my head. Since he was going out of his way to play the helpful corner policeman, I decided to take him up on it. If Chaney'd wanted the "safe house" address of the detective agency, he no doubt already had it. He could have fished it out of the telegraph operator on Friday night. Or had the operator showed some sign of integrity?

No matter. A safe house was supposed to be a safe house. I jotted down the address for Kirk. Let the boss worry about it. Let the agency worry about something, for a change.

"I'll give you some money for shipping," I said.

"I'll have it added to your hotel bill," he said nonchalantly. "You'll be settling that up pretty soon, won't you?"

"Haven't thought about it."

"Well, it must be expensive to stay at the Briggs, when your purpose is gone."

He was a sharp one, alright. Slicker than Chaney, more reasonable on the surface. At the station that first morning, Kirk had kept Mad Dog Smithers leashed, but he hadn't retreated from the orders to interrogate newcomers. He'd been mannerly, but firm, with Grant and me, and even with Corman when the doctor had questioned him.

But if there was a difference between Kirk and Chaney, it was solely in their manner. *In their manners.* The fact was, Kirk was still hungry. He wanted to be sheriff one day. He'd already spoken of "my men" toting the trunk. In a way, I almost preferred Fred Chaney's crudeness. At least he rattled before he struck.

"I may be in town a while," I told him. "I'm still looking for old ballads."

"Not union songs, I hope," he said in a totally neutral voice.

So they still thought Grant and I were connected with the mine union? Didn't they know about O'Dell? Or had they managed to eliminate him, too? Surely I'd have heard. And yet Chaney had been so full of himself, so confident about having the town under wraps.

"Trouble?" asked Smithers, stepping into the office.

"Hardly," answered Kirk.

Over and over, they kept reminding me I was no threat to them. What had Chaney said? *Josh Kirk can damn well take care of any little kindling flares up*. The worst of it was, they might just be right. There were so many of them, and only one of me.

Smithers moved closer, until the ex-blackleg was almost leaning on me. I felt like the big boys were bearing down with all their weight, and I was on the bottom. I could understand why Clair Bascomb tried so hard to keep the outside world, the coal camp grime and Fred Chaney and his ilk, out of her dollhouse.

"Anything come in on the train?" Kirk asked Smithers.

"Nothing not run-of-the-mine," said Smithers.

"The sheriff and Junior get off okay?"

"Yeah."

"Let's hope Junior stays away a while." Something in Kirk's voice told me he hoped Chaney would stay away a while, too. "I bet the sheriff will burn up Wheeling tonight."

"Bet he will," mumbled Smithers.

I thought of Clair again, of how she and Ben McGraw had described Chaney's tastes, his *fancies*. Even I knew that Wheeling, in the West Virginia panhandle between Ohio and Pennsylvania, had a reputation for high-rolling gambling, and around gamblers, flocked women, whores, I supposed. There was no great mystery why Wheeling was a magnet to the sheriff.

I felt Smithers' yellow eyes on me, as if he wanted to know why I was standing around taking up space.

"Good day," said Kirk, all manners as I went out the door.

When I reached the corner of Briggs Boulevard, I turned back to see if Smithers or another deputy was tailing me. Small fish swim scared. But they hadn't bothered.

I still wanted that bath I hadn't gotten, but I decided to skip it and keep working. I'd go check out the bakery before returning to the hotel, even though I wasn't sure what I'd ask. Still, the Italian bakers were the only lead I hadn't followed yet. I remembered Grant had stopped and studied the Blind Spring Bakery on our Thursday night walk. Had he known the bakers were close to Gatini?

It was early afternoon by the time I got there. I circled the bakery, pulling at doors and peering in windows, but the building was quiet and locked tight. Giving up, I walked back to the house behind the place. It was a comfortable two-story affair that looked as if it had been there long before Briggs and Company.

A round woman with curly iron-colored hair opened the door. She eyed me like she suspected I was a gangster or something while I hemmed and hawed the folklorist line. When I saw she wasn't following me, I put it more bluntly. "My name's Bill Edmonson. I've been told Alberto Gatini used to rent a room here."

She held up an index finger as a sign for me to wait, then closed the door and left me standing on the porch. A minute later, a young man in a white shirt was inspecting me, and then he led me back through the house into a small dining room where half a dozen people were crowded around a small table. The dishes in front of them showed traces of spaghetti sauce, and they all turned my way when I entered, as if I were a dangerous intruder.

The young man said something to a gaunt gray-haired man at the head of the table. The only word I picked up was "Papa." The rest was in rapid Italian.

"Bill Edmonson," said the old man in an accent so thick I almost didn't recognize my own name.

I nodded, and he looked to the young man. His son, I supposed. Whatever Papa said to him was in Italian, too. This time I recognized the words "Frank Grant."

"When we heard about Grant's death, we thought you might come," said the son.

24

The tiny dining room seemed to get bigger after Mama Mazzillo, the woman who'd answered my knock, herded everyone out but the old man, the son, and me. As they left us, they each grabbed plates and silverware. The smell of spicy tomato sauce stayed in the room even after Mama and her crew were through with their clearing.

The old man—he must have been in his seventies—motioned me to take a chair between him at one end and the son at the other. "Wine?" he offered.

The son slid a glass of red liquid in front of me before I could say no. I took a small sip, then just played with the stem, wanting to keep my head clear. Something made me recall Clair Bascomb's offer of wine on Sunday afternoon, and how I'd turned it down, only to accept it later. Stephen O'Dell had informed me Grant never turned down booze. If he was in a position to look down on me, Grant was probably laughing his head off. Hell, he was probably howling about all sorts of things I'd done since Thursday night.

Father and son seemed to be stalling, waiting for me to take the lead, so I tried to kick things off. "I'm looking for old stories. Someone told me about the murder of a prospector years ago, and how Alberto Gatini was arrested for it. They say Gatini rented a room from you. Some people believe he's innocent, and I wanted to hear what you have to say. You seem to have met Frank Grant. I was working with him."

"Is true," said Papa Mazzillo, rubbing at the long line of his jaw.

"Papa doesn't speak much English," explained the son in clear, second-generation American. "But he'll understand the gist of what you say. It just takes him a while to translate in his head."

"So Grant was here?"

The son nodded.

"Thursday night?" I asked.

He nodded again.

I could tell this was going to be a lot more work than getting Suze Chester's mouth rolling. The Mazzillos actually appeared frightened by me.

"Grant must have come here late," I said. "I was with him until after midnight."

"It was about one o'clock on Thursday night, Friday morning," said the son, twisting the dark hair above his ear. "We work nights at the bakery. It's cooler, and the bread's fresh for morning."

"We saw your lights that night. Why'd Grant stop in? I assume it was to ask about Gatini."

Rather than answer, the son spoke more Italian to his papa. It was like he was waiting for some kind of signal from the old man before proceeding.

Papa stared my way and said, "Detector," coming down hard on the first syllable of the word.

"So, you're a detective, like Grant?" asked the son.

"I said I was working with him," I answered, slowly and coldly. Grant sure hadn't done much to maintain our cover, I thought. He'd let both the widow and the Italians know who we were. How many others had he confided in?

"He did tell us he had an assistant, a Bill Edmonson," said the son. "How do we know you're him?"

"Top-notch question. Wish I could answer it. My name's not tattooed on my chest. My pockets aren't filled with affadavits. If you have doubts about me, check with the sheriff's office. Chaney, Kirk, Smithers, none of those guys have much use for me. They've not-so-politely suggested I get out of town."

"Chaney, Kirk," mumbled Papa Mazzillo, following the names with what I could only guess was a string of Neapolitan obscenities.

The son looked to the father again for direction. Finally, he said, "You're right. Grant wanted to know about Alberto. We . . ." Then they stared at each other for a long, dark moment.

"You what?"

"We called him in. . . . We called you in."

"You're the ones?"

"Yes."

"You might not believe this, but I didn't know. Grant didn't tell me."

"Mr. Grant was apparently an honorable man. We asked him not to let anyone know who he was working for, and it seems he didn't."

"What are you people so scared of?" I asked.

There was more Italian spoken between them, and then the son spoke to me again. "We wrote the detective agency after Alberto was convicted. We should have done it earlier, but we believed the jury had to find him innocent. When Grant contacted us, we told him Alberto was to be taken to prison this week. We thought it would be today or tomorrow. When they took him last Thursday, it surprised us all."

"When you say 'we,' who do you mean? Your family?"

"Our family, and the church."

"The Catholic church here in Blind Spring?"

"Yes. It was Papa's idea originally. He and Alberto were close friends. They knew some of the same places in the old country. In the evening, when Alberto came home from the mines, before we started baking, they'd sit and talk together. After they arrested Alberto, Papa was never the same. He couldn't understand how a jury had found him guilty. It was then that he went to the priest. We provided some of the money, but most of it came from a special, secret collection to clear Alberto's name. Everyone gave, the Italians—there aren't many of us—and the Irish miners, everyone."

Christ. I took a sip of wine.

"We simply couldn't stand the idea of Alberto being hanged for something he didn't do. We felt guilty we hadn't helped him before. We should have gotten him a better attorney. We should have done so many things. Now what? Grant is dead."

"Leaving me with two murders to solve," I said. "You've got to fill me in. Did anything unusual happen when Grant came to visit you? Was a deputy on his heels? Was anyone loitering outside the bakery while he was here?"

Papa was shaking his head no. The son said, "Nothing unusual. Grant came in about one o'clock, introduced himself, and asked some questions. He wanted to know if Alberto had ever discussed the prospector's death. We told him he hadn't, except to say it happened when he was away from the old mine and that he'd been very upset about it. This Scott seems to have been very good to him."

"How long did Grant stay Thursday night?"

"An hour or so. We were working while we talked. A batch of bread was going into the oven when he entered, and it was out before he left. I looked out the back door myself, and I didn't see anyone out there. We worried about him being followed. We were—we are—very nervous about being the ones who called you in."

"I can tell. Did he mention where he was going when he left here?"

"No. He stepped outside, lit a cigarette, and began walking away."

"Which way did he go?"

"Toward the Briggs Hotel. At least, I assumed that's where he was going. We knew you were staying there."

"How long had Gatini rented a room from you?"

"Ever since we moved to town."

"When was that?"

"We came to Blind Spring in March, two years ago, 1921."

"Any particular reason you picked Blind Spring to open a bakery in?" I recalled asking Clair Bascomb almost the same question.

"The family was in Philadelphia, all of us doing different jobs, when I saw a piece in the newspaper advertising buildings to lease and business opportunities in Murry County, West Virginia. I showed it to Papa and my younger brother. Papa was a baker in the old country. He often talked of wanting to open a bakery. We all pooled our savings and moved here. We weren't disappointed. There's money to be made in Blind Spring, if you work hard. That's why we came. This is America, isn't it?"

"I don't know. Anyway, you leased the bakery building from Timothy Briggs, right?"

"Briggs, no," said Papa Mazzillo.

"No?"

"We lease the building and this house from Sheriff Chaney," said the son.

"From Fred Chaney? Is that why you're so afraid? Do you think he might toss you out if you challenge his arrest of Gatini?"

"We worry about the sheriff, but our first lease was for three years, until next March. We have the option to renew it. Dr.

Corman specified that the sheriff has to honor any agreements he made."

"Anders Corman? Timothy Briggs' doctor? What's he have to do with it?"

"When we moved here, we leased from Dr. Corman. Now we pay Sheriff Chaney."

I was as surprised as I'd been when he told me my employers were the Roman Catholic congregation. On the train that first morning, as we'd pulled into Blind Spring, Corman hadn't indicated he was much involved with Blind Spring. He'd made a point, in fact, of saying only a wealthy man, like Timothy Briggs, could have pulled off the enterprise.

"Was Corman the one who put the ad in the Philadelphia paper in 1921?" I asked.

"Yes. Then, last fall, Sheriff Chaney acquired the property."

"All this time I've thought Briggs owned the entire town. He certainly acts like does."

Papa understood me well enough to shake his head no.

"I imagine Mr. Briggs owns most of Blind Spring," said the son. "But I know Dr. Corman owns several large properties. I don't know what Sheriff Chaney owns. The doctor used to own more than he does now. From what I understand, he's been selling his holdings over the years, mostly to Mr. Briggs, except for our buildings."

"Huh," I mumbled, glancing around the dining room. The walls felt like they were closing in again.

"Is all this important?" asked the son.

"I don't know. Could be. I just hadn't expected it. When exactly did Chaney take over your lease?"

"Late in the fall of 1922. It wasn't very long after Alberto was arrested."

"Has Chaney caused you any problems since he's been your landlord?"

"Nothing serious."

"What's serious?"

"He reminds us he's around. Once in a while, he might come in, look around, and walk off with a loaf of bread. That's about it. He's different from Dr. Corman, that's all. The doctor was always very much a gentleman to us."

"He's a gentleman to everyone," I agreed. "Look, are any of Gatini's things still around? Is there anything that might tell me something about him?"

"Only his clothes. We put them up in the attic in case he ever needs them. He didn't own very much. He had a small bank account, always donated money to the church, always sent some back to relatives in the old country."

Papa Mazzillo must have grasped we were talking about money. "You stay work for us?" he asked. "You still have money?"

"I'm still working. Everything's alright. The money's holding up," I told him.

"What you do now?" asked the old man.

"I'm not sure." I took another sip of wine.

"Must be hard, this being a detective," said the son. "I'm glad I'm a baker."

Too damn hard, I thought, but what I said was cheerier. "Save Gatini's clothes. With any luck, he may need them again."

With any luck.

As if luck was something their money could buy.

25

As I left the Mazzillo house, I was thinking about luck. Or rather, about how much of it I was going to need.

On the way out to the street, I stopped at the back door of the bakery and scouted around to see what Grant would have seen when he left the place in the last hours of his life. There was a little roof overhanging the doorstep, and I pictured Grant standing there, lighting his cigarette before launching out into the dark.

What had happened then?

If I hadn't come to them, would the Mazzillos and the congregation simply have washed their hands of the whole affair? After bringing us to town, would they have just let me flounder on my own?

Hell, the detective agency wasn't doing much better.

Feeling the plague of despair descending again, I decided to keep moving rather than go back to the hotel just yet. I let my feet pick the direction, while my head wandered somewhere else. I don't know how other people's minds work, but that's how mine's always worked best. I always was a walk-the-floor sort. Thinking back on Grant's perpetual motion on Thursday, I guessed he was, too.

Thinking about Grant really got me going. I knew so damn little about him. Christ, I'd found out as much, or more, about Blind Spring's other victims, Scott and Gatini, as I had about Grant. Strange. I mean, how old had Grant been? Where was he born? Had he ever married? Did he have children out there someplace? Had he ever had a job other than being a detective?

Maybe detectives didn't ever show more about themselves than they had to. Maybe it was like the introduction to the ballad book put it: *The teller of the tale has no role in it.* Not even if his life was in danger.

In any case, what I knew about Grant could be summed up fast. He smoked, he cussed, and he never turned down a drink. He had a temper you didn't want to cross. He alternated between lecture and silence. Then, again, lectures didn't really tell you much about a person. He read newspapers and had an interest in history, especially industrial history. He was always searching for those thin, almost invisible strings that hold hot-air balloons to the ground. He'd been to coal towns before, but he'd never been to New Mexico. He was "honorable," to use Mazzillo's word. So honorable and secretive, he hadn't even bothered to tell me—his partner—who we were working for, because that's the way they'd wanted it. He could be a "rough bastard," according to Stephen O'Dell, as if I hadn't known. He slipped on a different personality when he had to. He dropped his cover when it wasn't doing him any good. He went about by himself, and he'd paid the price for it. Fell into a coal car, claimed Fred Chaney.

Saturday night, Dr. Corman had said he had little use for Dr. Freud and the new psychology, but some analyst would have had a career-making study in Frank Grant.

Anders Corman. There, too, was a subject worth study. The Mazzillos saw him as a gentleman, a man who'd given them a chance to set up shop in Blind Spring. I didn't know how to view him, or all his talk about my "destiny" being to work for

Timothy Briggs, or his misleading Grant and me about the extent of his interest in the town. So bland on the surface.

What was it Clair had said? *Everything's different beneath the surface, isn't it?* And what had the sheriff told Junior? "I'm no Corman lover."

Some goddamn mine town Grant had left me in! It was virtually impossible to know what you could say to who about whom. And why was Chaney so certain Blind Spring was safe in his absence? Maybe Josh Kirk really had the smarts in the operation, like some people said. Or maybe—it had crossed my mind earlier—maybe they'd uncovered Stephen O'Dell.

I looked up the hill at the company houses lining the street. From where I stood, I could see both the road in front of them and the rows of frame outhouses behind them.

Sometimes that's what happens when you allow your feet to make your choices for you. Without thinking, you end up where your mind was leading you all along. *Welcome home, Professor Freud.*

A bunch of kids were playing ball in the street, but I didn't spot any cops, so I hiked up the grade to Kayce Powell's house. When I got there, Polly Powell, a broom in her hand, opened the door. Her baby was crawling around on the floor behind her. When I asked about Kayce, she gave me a weird stare and said, "Why, he's working, don't you know? He's at the East Works, like every other day."

"I never thought about it," I managed to mumble.

"He should be home in an hour or so, after the shift changes," she said, shutting the door without inviting me in.

I crossed the street and sat on the hillside below the ridgeline that ran over to McGraw's stable. Waiting for Kayce Powell, I watched the kids play ball and wondered which of them had slipped Powell's note into my hand on Friday morning.

They were batting uphill, which meant they had to hit a real good shot to get anywhere. But hitting the other way would have meant letting the ball get away more times than anyone would've wanted to chase it. The sun was leaning west, striking the fielders' faces.

Always my favorite game, baseball. It was how I'd spent entire weeks of my younger summers. Hell, *younger* years. Although I felt like I was aging fast, I was still only twenty-one and counting. Twenty-one, and wishing I was playing ball in the street instead of doing what I was supposed to be doing, whatever that was.

A fat kid hit the taped-up ball with all his might and it sailed over the fielders' heads, up the slope, and landed just below me. "Foul ball," cried one boy, who then looked at me like he expected me to throw the ball back to him.

As I retrieved it, I suddenly had a stronger urge to play, and they didn't complain when I joined them in the street. When the black-faced miners started coming home, I was on my toes, squinting into the sun and facing downhill toward home plate. Now and then, I glanced over my shoulder to make sure I didn't miss Kayce Powell.

Many of the miners were scarcely older than the kids I was playing ball with. A lot of them were younger than me, much younger than the century. Maybe I was feeling guilty, but I sensed envy in their eyes as they watched us having fun.

Finally, I saw Kayce Powell and stepped away from the ballgame to catch him before he could disappear inside.

"What the hell are you doing?" he asked, irritated. "You ought to be more careful. What if one of the deputies saw you here?"

"I . . . I was just wondering if O'Dell's okay."

"What's it matter to you? Why wouldn't he be?"

"Chaney's gone to Wheeling, and he told me the union organizer was taken care of. I didn't know what he meant. I guess I started worrying."

"Hasn't O'Dell been in touch with you?"

"No."

"He's been trying."

"I haven't been around the hotel much in the last couple days. What's he want?"

Kayce shifted his lunch pail nervously from one hand to another. "He's learned a few things you might want to know. Let him tell you himself."

"Where do I find him?"

He stood silent a moment, then said, "Let him find you. You be behind the hotel, at the kitchen door, when the dining room closes tonight. I'll tell him and he'll arrange a ride or some way to take you to him. Now, get away from here!" He opened his door and hurried in.

I hadn't reached the foot of the hill before I saw why he'd rushed me away. I heard an automobile and, when I turned around, the kids were scurrying out of the street so the car could pass. It stopped when it got even with me.

"You lost?" asked Josh Kirk.

Next to him, at the steering wheel, was Deputy Smithers, anger in his eyes as usual.

"I'm just going about my business, seeking songs," I said. "You've got to do a lot of legwork in this racket."

"What racket would that be?"

"Folkloring."

"We've shipped Professor Grant's trunk home for you," said Kirk. "You want a lift back to the hotel? I trust that's where you're going."

"I'll hoof it."

"Have it your way," said Kirk, and Smithers accelerated them away.

I was tired and hot, and it was a healthy hike to the hotel, but spending more time with Kirk and Smithers wasn't my idea of a pleasant summer afternoon. I'd have rather played baseball in a blizzard.

26

I was halfway back to the Briggs Hotel when I noticed the wagon inching along beside me. Glancing over, I saw a few baskets of strawberries in the bed and, in the driver's seat, Moses, wearing the same patched overalls he'd worn on Saturday.

He waved me up onto the seat next to him, and then urged the horses on faster. I thought maybe he was taking me someplace for more target practice, but we ended up at McGraw's stable.

As we entered, Ben McGraw was leaning on the anvil, his back to us, jawing about something with Suze Chester, who sat in the rocking chair next to the potbellied stove. Whatever they'd been discussing, they stopped when they saw us, or when they saw me.

"You're all dressed up to come to town, huh?" I asked Suze.

She was definitely outfitted in her best, from her well-shined black shoes to her veiled purple hat.

"I've been to the courthouse," she answered. "I took the train to the county seat this morning and just got back."

"Yeah? Why?"

"I told you I'd search through Scott's things to see if there was anything important."

"What'd you find?"

She reached into her small suitcase of a handbag, pulled out some papers, and handed them over to me. Some were loose and some were in soiled envelopes, but they'd all obviously been folded and unfolded many times, read over and over again. They were so worn that they were ready to tear with the slightest mishandling. I placed them atop the cold stove and scanned them one at a time, trying to treat them gently. Once I was through the papers the first time, I went back again and read them more closely. The whole time, Suze, McGraw, and Moses silently watched me.

By and large, the documents appeared to be geologist's reports. One was dated October 17, 1917, and another, eight months later—June something—the date had been blotted out and the handwriting was worse than my own scrawl—June something, 1918. As best I could make out, Suze had been accurate when she'd said the coal from Scott's mine was "harder" than bituminous yet "softer" than anthracite. The geologist responsible for the reports seemed to find it marketable, especially considering its location.

For laymen, the geologist had provided a summary of his findings and had attached it to the June 1918 report:

> Given its location on undeveloped land near the Shawnee–Potomac Railroad mainline, Lancelot Scott's mine may have real potential. It would appear to have a seam of reasonable depth. A similar site is east of the small village of Blind Spring, and it appears to have as much economic value. There may be other possible mining areas. Local residents feel there is iron ore in

> the vicinity. This, too, is reasonable, but whether the iron ore is of sufficient quality and quantity requires further study. Adding to the feasibility of capital investment are the forests of the valley, which could be timbered for rapid return. Arrangements could be made with the railroad to expand the present tracks.
>
> Nate Corman

"God," I said, dropping the report on top of the other papers.

"Doesn't the name mean something?" asked Suze Chester.

"Anders Corman is Timothy Briggs's doctor," I said. "I've heard he owned various properties around town. I take it this Nate Corman is one of the men Scott called in?"

She nodded. "That's why I went to the courthouse. I thought the deeds might show something. I didn't tell you ahead of time, because I didn't know if it would amount to anything. You see, those years are all confusing to me. I didn't keep track of everything Scott did, and, to us back then, a rich man from Philadelphia was just a rich man from Philadelphia, whether his name was Briggs or Corman."

"I can understand that, especially considering the fact that Timothy Briggs was the one who eventually moved in and started up operations. What'd you find in the courthouse?"

"Briggs never bought an acre of Blind Spring until February 1919. That'd be six months after Scott was murdered, in August. The one who was buying up all the land was this Anders Corman. I figure he's the brother of the geologist."

"Some relative, no doubt."

"It all happened so fast, and I was mourning Scott. I guess I just didn't know all the in's and out's. But, on the same day in October, five years ago, this Corman bought both Charlie Happersalk's property, which is Briggs' West Works now, and Harry Mays' property, which is the East Works now. He was buying up everything else he could, too."

"So, Briggs wasn't here then, but his agents were, his spirit was," I said, repeating what Suze and the whiskey man had told me on Saturday. And John Summerset had added something else. The word had been out in 1918 that a wealthy Philadelphian wanted *all* of Blind Spring, not only part of it.

Goddamn lying bastard. First, the Mazzillos had told me Dr. Corman owned a good bit of the town, and now Suze was telling me he'd owned more than a good bit, that he'd damn near owned it all at one time. The son of a bitch had misled the hell out of Grant and me on the train. He'd played with words, covering up his real interest. No wonder he'd complained about the poor accommodations at the hotel in the county seat. He remembered the place well from his early visits.

"Okay," I said. "You've told me Charlie Happersalk isn't around anymore. How about this other guy, this Mays? He must have sold Corman a big tract of land."

Ben McGraw piped up. "You probably seen Harry around town. He's always moaning, 'Lose your railroad, lose your wife.'"

"'Only Jesus Christ was great'?"

"That's the fellow."

"Where does he live?"

"Up the hill, about a mile above the miners' houses, in his family's old homestead."

"I thought you said he sold it," I said to Suze.

"He sold all of it outright but a couple acres around the house. Maybe Harry has a sentimental side, who knows? Anyway, according to the deed, he kept the right to use the house until he died."

"Lucky he did that," said McGraw.

"Why?"

"Where else would he live?"

"He should be able to lead a fairly comfortable life, with the money he got for his land," I said.

"He didn't get paid as much as you'd think," said Suze.

"None of them boys did," said McGraw. "They was big pieces of mountain land mostly, and no one judged they was worth much. Most of them didn't get twenty-five dollars an acre overall. Seems like a big enough offer, though, when you ain't seen so much cash."

McGraw, it hit me, was the man who'd later refused to sell his own family homeplace to Briggs. And he'd kept his blacksmith shop while Blind Spring grew up around it.

"The Mays family used to be prominent here," said Suze. "They owned the flour mill. Harry's granddaddy was involved in Murry County politics."

"Business went sour," said McGraw. "Everything tumbled downhill full-throttle till Harry got the chance to unload the place and make some money off Briggs, or this Corman fellow, or whoever the hell it was bought it."

I pictured Harry Mays, his long uncombed white hair, his gray wool all-weather coat. "Still looks like he's tumbling downhill to me. How'd his brain end up so addled?"

"Well, for a time, him and his wife—Harry was married then—they left here," said McGraw. "I heard they went to Huntington and lived in a big hotel or someplace. They just squandered their money. Drinking, gambling, him buying that woman all sorts of stuff. Then the cash got low, and she run off with some other man, and soon Harry's back here in Blind Spring. Moved right back into the homeplace. That was two years ago, and he ain't done nothing but drink and moan his singsong ever since. 'Lose your railroad.' He lost his, I guess."

"Sounds like I'd better go see him. At the least, he'd know who was putting pressure on him and the others to sell their land five years ago."

"If he can recall five years back. You seen him. You know he ain't going to be an easy one to get nothing out of."

"John Summerset knows him," said Suze. "I bet he'd go with

you. He'd make it a lot simpler. He could take along a jar of whiskey and bribe Harry's mouth open. Harry'd do anything for a drink. Summerset talks his lingo, too, if you get me. Even if I don't approve of John Summerset, he's like me on one account. He'd go far out of his way to learn who murdered Scott."

"You're probably right," I said, thinking back to the whiskey man's description of Scott's body and how he didn't want Suze to see the prospector in such shape.

"He might come down to town tonight," said McGraw. "He usually does."

"I . . . I've got to be somewhere else tonight," I said, remembering I was supposed to make connections with Stephen O'Dell.

"Just as well," said Suze. "I'd like to talk to John Summerset myself. Moses and me will stop and see him on our way home. This has waited five years, it'll hold for another night. Anyway, you've got to do it properly and not scare Harry off. Let's say, unless you hear from me otherwise, you meet Summerset here tomorrow about noon."

"Time's right," said McGraw. "Harry Mays ain't likely to be an early riser."

"Tuesday at noon," I agreed. "I'll be here."

Suze pushed herself up from the rocking chair and walked over to the woodstove and collected Scott's papers, folding them on the same dirty crease lines and burying them in her bag. Then she turned back to face me. "There's one more thing I noticed in the courthouse."

"What?"

"The very same lawyer they hired to defend Alberto Gatini was the one whose name was on a lot of the deeds when Corman bought up land."

"Shit!" exploded McGraw.

"Worse," said Suze, motioning for Moses. "We'll go find Summerset."

McGraw and I watched Suze and Moses walk out the stable door and climb up onto the wagon seat. "Sounds bad for this fellow Corman," said McGraw as the wagon rolled off.

"I don't know. Could sound worse than it really is. There's no crime in land speculation. It wasn't murder."

"Might have been."

"You've got to be careful about jumping to conclusions." Hell, I sounded like Frank Grant.

"I say it sounds bad." He reached into his pocket, pulled out his flask, and unscrewed the lid. "Want a nip?"

"Sure."

"I knew when I saw you that you boys wasn't interested in no old ballads," he said as he handed me the flask.

27

The deputy on the porch watched me as I left the hotel Monday night, but he didn't bother to warn me about Blind Spring's dangers. I headed around the corner of the building, out of his sight, and then ducked around the next corner and hurried along until I was behind the kitchen. There, I leaned against the wall, staying to the shadows as best I could, listening to the dishwashers clatter the pots and dishes around. It didn't take a genius to figure out they were in a hurry to call it quits.

So was I. *For I'm wearied wi huntin and ſain wad lie down,* as Lord Randall would have told his mother.

Earlier, I'd almost fallen asleep in the bathtub, once I'd finally climbed into the tub of warm water I'd wanted all day. Undressing, I'd imagined I could still smell Clair Bascomb on me. What would my Catholic employers have said to that? For that matter, what would my Protestant relatives have said? Hell, most of them had probably done worse in their time.

I'd rubbed the soap against my skin, then leaned back in the wet warmth, thinking how I wanted to see her again. Love? Not quite. After all, adventure and women were what I'd wanted out of detective work, not being a tired flatfoot. And, so far, she was the closest I'd come to what I'd been after.

My mind was still on Sunday's ferris wheel ride when the kitchen workers started coming out the back door of the Briggs Hotel—the same back door Grant must have exited from on Thursday night. All but three or four of the black men in their white uniforms began walking away. The others seemed to be waiting for something, glancing my way now and again as they loitered outside the kitchen door.

Finally, I heard the sounds of a rattletrap coming up the street. One of the kitchen workers waved for me to join them as they moved toward the noise. Soon we'd climbed in and the old car was winding through the streets of Blind Spring. Because I'd totally lost any sense of direction, I wasn't really sure where we were, even when we got there.

All but one of the hotel workers evaporated in the darkness as soon as the car doors opened. There were no streetlights, and not even as much light leaking from the few buildings as at the company houses. Up the dirt road from us, I could barely make out the shapes of small houses that looked to be little more than shanties.

"This way," directed the remaining man.

I followed him twenty yards or so toward a larger structure that had probably been a farmhouse in the old days. We circled around the back, then went down steps of mountain stone and into a dark cellar. The damn thing could have been a mine shaft.

My guide left me standing inside the door and walked over to a table where a group of other men sat. A wave of laughter rose when they spotted him. I couldn't help wondering whether they were laughing at me.

The tables in the dingy cellar were jammed close together, leaving a small open space in the dimly lit center of the floor. The clinking of glasses made me look around the speakeasy for the bar. When I found it, I found Stephen O'Dell.

O'Dell was deep in conversation with two Negroes, one leaning on the rough-hewn counter on either side of him. Trying to copy Grant's confident strut, I walked over to them. One of the men glanced at me as if to ask, What are you doing here?

"Just the man I've been waiting on," said O'Dell when I reached him. Turning back to the men, he said, "Stay true. Hold the line. Give the strike a chance. Time's the main thing."

His style was low-key, but they appeared to be hanging on his every word as if it was the gospel. Eventually, they went off to a corner table and I asked, "Are they coal miners?"

"Yeah." I could almost feel the tiredness in his voice. "There's those who say you can't trust Negroes and foreigners to keep loyal in a strike, but I've never had any trouble. Take those guys—they've worked in mines or done tunnel work all their lives. They've got as much at stake as anyone else."

"So, you're gearing up for a strike?"

"Yeah. It's as ready as done. There's no better time, with Chaney out of town, Briggs Junior gone, and the old man ailing. They won't know what hit them. It starts tonight, with the next shift, in fact."

"I wondered if you knew Chaney had gone to Wheeling."

"Hell, I could tell you where he's staying, if you really want to know. What'd he tell you when you drove to the station with him this morning?"

"You really do have your sources, don't you?"

"I told you Friday night I did."

"The sheriff said he deserved a vacation and there was no reason why he shouldn't take one. He said Josh Kirk could take care of any little thing that popped up, and seemed to believe Blind Spring's union organizer had been taken care of. I wondered if you were alright."

"What's this sudden concern for me?" asked O'Dell. "You didn't want any part of me before."

"That's not what I said, and you know it. All I was trying to get across was that I'm here to find a murderer or two, and you're here to organize miners. I don't see how mixing the two helps me. I've got enough problems."

"The two are already mixed up. Haven't you figured out why they killed Frank?"

"Not exactly, except the cops are always asking me what my connection with the union is."

"There it is, wrapped up for you, don't you see? They did away with Frank Grant because they thought he was me. They're only putting up with you because they don't think you can do much on your own, and they probably want to see what contacts you make. It was stupid to go to Kayce Powell's house today."

"There wasn't anybody following me. Look, how are you so sure that's why Grant was murdered?"

"One of the miners told me."

"Told you what?"

"This man was working the night shift at the East Works, and early Friday morning, when there weren't many people out and around, he was with the crew at the tipple, loading cars. He claims a sheriff's car drove up and three men got out. One of them, he was sure, was Chaney. He couldn't quite see who the deputy with him was. The other fellow walked like he was maybe in handcuffs, and could have had a gun pointed at his back. Anyway, they walked up the tracks a ways, into the dark and away from the tipple. When they came back and climbed in the car, there were only two of them. It was the same train they found Frank's body on."

I didn't say anything for a long while. I guess O'Dell must have noticed how white I was. "You want a drink?" he asked.

When I didn't answer, he called to the bartender and ordered me a whiskey. I took a big gulp and didn't even feel the bite.

"So, whose side are you on now?"

"What can I say? I'm not against you, but actively lining up with you would only bring Chaney's boys down harder on me. I already feel their pressure. God, do I feel their pressure."

"You haven't seen pressure yet," said O'Dell, his voice heating up a little. "The strike'll really bring things to a head. I know what side Frank would be on."

"I'm not Grant," I said. "Grant's dead. I've got to do this my own way. Don't you understand that much? So, what's going to happen? What can I expect? I've got to know."

O'Dell took a sip of bootleg, and, when he finally spoke, his voice was cooler. "Whatever people say about me, I run things careful, conservative. I've learned my lessons over the years. Any violence will begin on the other side. There'll be no snipers shooting into the mines, no tipples burnt, unless they shoot first. If they bring in the Baldwin-Felts dicks for added force, like they did in Mingo County, things could get rough. Frank hated the Baldwin-Felts boys as much as I do. He didn't believe hired guns should be allowed to call themselves detectives. . . . Anyway, you just have to play these things by ear. The miners will simply stay home, away from the mines. In a day or two, if there's been no response, the women will go downtown and see what kind of reception they get in the company stores. That'll tip us off. If there still hasn't been a response by Thursday or Friday, we'll do some kind of a mass rally. Maybe we'll hold it outside the Briggs Hotel."

"What do you mean when you say a response?"

"It could be that Timothy Briggs invites some of us to meet with him to negotiate. It could be violence. It could be they'll evict the strikers from the company properties."

"I've seen Timothy Briggs. I wouldn't bet he's going to leap out of his bed and rush to the bargaining table."

"Neither would I," O'Dell almost whispered.

"Do the men know they could get thrown out of their homes?"

"I don't dwell on it, but, sure, they know. Some of them have been through this before. During the big Pullman strike in the 'nineties, George Pullman played company-house games. He raised rents at the same time he cut wages, saying there wasn't any connection between who he hired and who he rented to. Right here in West Virginia they tossed miners out three years ago during the mine wars, but they argued the case different. Judge Damron ruled the strikers couldn't stay in company houses even if they *paid* their rent. He said the mine owner/miner relationship was one of master/servant, not landlord/tenant. It's the kind of thing that makes radicals of men like General Coxey."

"You mean Coxey's Army?"

O'Dell's red head nodded. "Jacob Sechler Coxey, back in March 1894, a depression year. Gay nineties, bunk. Coxey led a bunch of unemployed veterans to Washington, demanding veterans benefits, more money in circulation, and public works jobs for all able men. They started their march at Massillon, Ohio, only a hundred miles from Warren G. Harding's hometown. Funny, if Harding hadn't been prosperous, he might have been with them."

Suddenly I felt like I was hearing one of Grant's history lectures. "Did you see Coxey's Army?" I asked.

"Yeah. I was just a kid, and my uncle took me with him to deliver a wagonload of food to them. Hundreds of them were on the C and O Canal towpath, all heading to the U.S. Capitol. They were quite an attraction, and people fed them all along the way. In Shawnee, they collected funds by charging admission to their campsite."

"They arrested him for conspiracy or something, didn't they?"

"Hell, no. They arrested Coxey for walking on the grass in Washington. That really made him a radical. He's still going strong."

"What made you a radical?" I asked.

O'Dell straightened up and dropped some money on the bar.

He took a step toward the door, then turned back. "Keep your mouth shut about the strike, and about me."

"If I learn anything you can use," I said, "I'll find a way to let you know."

"Obliged."

I watched him saunter to the door, but the fact he was leaving was forgotten as soon as he was out of sight. Instead, I worried about myself. If Chaney and his goons had picked up Grant and taken him to the East Works to beat him up, where did that leave me? They might pick me up at any moment. How do you catch a sheriff? I wondered. How do you stop the goons?

A vibrating guitar note pierced through the heavy smoke in the dark cellar. As if it was what they'd been waiting for, couples immediately jumped to the clear area of the floor and began slow-dragging to the bluesy tune.

I ordered another whiskey, and when the bartender put it in front of me, I reached into my pocket for my wallet. It wasn't until I'd handed him a dollar bill that I looked down and saw Grant's battered billfold in my hand. Quickly, I stuck it back in my coat pocket and took a swig.

"Sometimes I want to leave here,
Sometimes I want to stay. . . ."

The singer filled in between lines with stinging, almost metallic guitar notes.

"Sometimes I want to stay here,
Sometimes I want to leave. . . ."

I certainly knew the feeling. There'd been plenty of times in the last few days when I'd considered just walking away from Blind Spring. At that moment, I wasn't even sure why I hadn't.

When the singer's song of indecision was over, the crowd gave him a hand and started yelling requests. Through the bodies on the dark dance floor, I could only get a glimpse of him, but when he began to sing again there was something familiar about both the voice and the song.

The lyrics were about riding into Briggs Town on a hellbound train, about the snarling guards at the depot, about the scrip for pay, the deep dangerous mine holes, the falling timber, the scramble for tips at the hotel, the workaday emptiness of the place. The melody was the same one Timothy Briggs had ordered Simpson to perform on Friday afternoon, but the words had been turned upside down and inside out. They were brutal instead of sunny, and the singer's voice got rougher, more ferocious, as he went on.

I could feel his anger from across the cellar, could sense it each time his right hand tugged at a string and the string rattled against the knife edge that his left hand held flush against the guitar's neck.

In the speakeasy, surrounded by his friends, Simpson couldn't get away with less than the truth.

28

The next morning, the street in front of the Briggs Hotel was lined with deputies who smoked and chatted, their eyes constantly on the move. It was obvious that no striking miner would be allowed anywhere near the place. I wondered how the cops would deal with me when it came time to go to McGraw's stable and meet the whiskey man for our trip to Harry the drunk's.

I was on the balcony, looking down on the milling mine guards when Simpson knocked at my door.

"Did you see Briggs' men out there?" I asked as soon as he was in the room and the door was shut.

"How could you miss them?"

"What have you heard? Are they stopping people and harassing them? Have they moved in on the strikers yet?"

"Nothing going on much, at least that I heard about, but I been here in the hotel since seven o'clock. When I come to work, the guards was running around like rabid possums, not sure what to do about the miners staying away from the mines."

"Mr. Briggs knows everything, I guess."

"Yeah," said Simpson. "I took him up a letter from Mr. O'Dell already, saying the union was ready to sit down and talk whenever he's willing."

"Is he willing?"

"Not yet, not yet." Simpson laughed softly. "He will be some day, according to Mr. O'Dell. What Mr. Briggs did was telegram Wheeling to call the sheriff back. Then he sent me down to get you."

"Does O'Dell know the sheriff's coming back?"

"Don't know. I haven't had no chance to get word to him."

"Maybe I can later," I said, thinking I'd go by the company houses on the way to Harry Mays'. "What's Briggs want with me?"

"Him and the doctor want to see you."

"I guess if I don't go up, they'll send some deputies to retrieve me."

"I guess they would."

"Let's get it over with."

I followed Simpson out the door, down the hall past the state rooms, and up the staircase. The *District*'s guard had been doubled, and both deputies reached for their guns when they saw us. They must have been scared as hell. Luckily, they realized we were on Briggs business when they recognized Simpson.

"Judging by all the guards around this place, there can't be many cops out on patrol," I said as we walked up the hall.

"There's enough of them."

Anders Corman answered my knock. Without greeting, he made room for me to step in, then slammed the door in Simpson's face. You could almost touch the doctor's anger and grab the gloomy air between the four walls.

"Goddamn miners are on strike," announced Corman as he plopped down in a chair beside the bed. "But you knew as much, didn't you?"

"Bastarding Bolshevikers," mumbled Timothy Briggs.

The old man was flat on his back, and his big head was the

only thing that showed. His voice sounded weaker than it had on Friday afternoon. Looking at him, I couldn't help recalling what the whiskey man and Suze Chester had said about his spirit being present in Blind Spring, even before he was. Briggs was still more spirit than flesh.

"You say the miners have struck?" I asked, playing along.

"You didn't know?" asked Corman.

"I keep telling everyone that Grant and I had nothing to do with the union."

I knew from Corman's eyes that he didn't believe me, but he said, "To a man, the miners didn't show up for work this morning."

"The sheriff must have been right about a union organizer in town."

"Goddamn Fred Chaney. He should never have gone away. He just wanted to feed his appetites. We've wired him, and he's supposed to be on his way back. If all goes well, he should be here in a few hours. He'll have to do his damndest to throw a scare into them and bust this strike."

"String them up . . . like baubly beads," mumbled the head on its pillow.

"Ignore Timothy," said Corman. "He was so upset that I was forced to give him a sedative. It was all I could do to stop him from climbing out of bed and leading an assault on the company houses himself. He's taking this personally, as he should, if you ask me. He's fighting the medication, but he'll drift off soon enough."

Always quick with the knockout drops, this physician. Briggs had called him a big medicine man on Friday, and he no doubt knew what he was talking about.

"Thy'll bobble," said Briggs, his voice dragging and becoming more distant. He wasn't sure what he was saying any longer, and neither was I.

"Where were you last night?" Corman asked. "The deputy saw you leave the hotel and you didn't return for hours."

"I went for a walk."

"You're always going for a walk, aren't you? Josh Kirk says you were over by the company houses yesterday."

"You have to get around and mix with the people to collect folklore."

"Will you drop this folklore stuff. I don't know why you're in town, but it's not for old ballads. I'll make it clear for you. We've suggested twice that it would be to your advantage to work for Timothy. Didn't you understand our offer? This is the last chance you'll get to accept it."

"What would I do for Mr. Briggs exactly?"

"Right now, you can be useful by simply walking around town as you have been. People have apparently gotten used to you. They talk to you, whether they believe you're collecting songs, or know you're after something else."

"What you want is a spy. You figure everyone is aware of Professor Grant's death, so no one would associate me with you boys."

"Call it spying if you like, but I can assure you that Timothy had nothing to do with Grant's unfortunate death, no matter what the local fools are saying. Why, they're only rumor-mongering. It's just how they reacted to the death of the prospector."

"I don't know why I should believe you."

"And am I to believe you? Do you think you've taken me in with this folklore thing? Let's face it, you've not been forthright."

"Neither have you. I understand your name's on a lot of deeds in the county courthouse. You were the one who actually brought Briggs here, weren't you? You've been selling him land for five years—land that you bought up cheap after Scott was murdered."

"What if I have? You look as if you have enough brains to realize that has nothing to do with anything else. There's no rift between Timothy and me. In fact, if you know so damn much, you must know I have very little property left here. By the time I leave Blind Spring this summer, our transactions for the rest of what I own will be complete."

"What will you do then? Look for a new place to buy up, and another rich patient back in Philadelphia to sell it to at a premium? Maybe Nate Corman, the famous geologist, will help you find your next investment."

"I'm sorry you think it's a crime to make money," said Corman. "Perhaps we believed you have more intelligence than you have."

"Sorry, sorra, sorro, sarru," moaned the head on the pillow, as if it was lost in the declensions of some long-lost Latin class.

I turned away from Corman and stared at the large map on the wall behind the desk. "Shows it all, doesn't it? The East Works, what used to be Harry Mays' land until you bought it, is actually bigger than the West Works, which used to be Charlie Happersalk's, isn't it?"

"East is west, and west is work, and ne'er the twine shill beep," said Timothy Briggs, another whistlestop closer to nirvana.

"Must be a piece of cake to negotiate land deals when you keep him in Neverland," I told Corman. "Must be as simple as dealing with Harry Mays over a whiskey jar."

"Where'd you grow up? In the gutter? How'd you get so cocky all of a sudden? You've got nothing to be cocky about. You're going to end up a loser, like those damn coal miners, unless you throw in with us. All we want you to do is circulate and tell us what people are saying and doing."

"I've got scruples, Doctor. You get it straight. I came here with Frank Grant and I'm not leaving this town until I find out who murdered him, and who murdered Lancelot Scott."

"What the hell do you care about Scott?"

"I'm a detective." There, I'd laid it out.

"Get out of here!" yelled Corman, losing the last of his composure.

I was crossing the carpet to the door when old man Briggs mumbled, "Outta hear ye, hear ye."

I fought to keep myself from hurrying as I walked to the stairs. Grant wouldn't have hurried. He'd have been as plodding—he would have stepped as hard—as a dinosaur. I even forced myself to say "Good day" to the deputies, like nothing was wrong.

On the third-floor landing, I took a deep breath and punched the elevator button. Down in the lobby, I asked for my messages at the desk. When the desk clerk came back empty-handed, I went to the dining room. No one was going to run me off. Not Corman, not Chaney, no one.

The ham and eggs didn't have much flavor that morning, or maybe my tastebuds weren't connected to my brain any longer. The whole time I chewed, facts, conversations, hearsay, impressions, and emotions rattled against their couplings like cars on a long freight.

Why didn't it get any easier the more I found out? Had I made a false move telling the doctor I was a detective?

It was too late to worry about it. All I could do was meet John Summerset and hope the whiskey man and I could make some sense out of Harry Mays. All I could do was keep working.

29

"Mr. Edmonson?" The desk clerk called to me as I headed through the lobby.

"Yes?"

"You received a telephone call while you were in the dining room. A Miss Bascomb," he said, a knowing glint in his eye. "She said we needn't bother to interrupt you, but she'd like you to return her call. Here's the number."

I called her from the public phone near the elevator. It could have been my imagination, but I sensed her voice brightened as soon as I introduced myself.

"Something wrong?" I asked.

"No, nothing." She stopped. "I . . . I'd just like to see you again. I have some things to tell you. . . . We have some things to talk about."

"What?"

"I . . . I'd rather not discuss them on the telephone. I've been thinking a lot about your visit on Sunday."

"So have I."

"You'll come, then?" she asked anxiously, as if maybe I wouldn't.

"Of course, but it may be a while. I've got some things to do first. It could be late this afternoon before I get there."

"I'll be here," she said. "I've no other plans for the day. I'll be free."

After I hung up, I thought about what she'd said. *I'll be free.* No other plans for the day. No excursion in a rich man's private railway car. Did that mean she wanted to see me? Well, there was no use reading anything into it. Something had simply happened that made her want to talk. Whatever it was, I felt like it was my job to listen.

I went out the door to the front porch, where three deputies were sitting, each with a shotgun leaning next to him. They scarcely glanced at me as I passed them. I was still small fish, as Sheriff Chaney had let me know, and his men weren't as worried about me, or whoever else might leave the Briggs Hotel, as they were about who might try to enter the joint that morning.

Clumps of deputies were still posted up and down the street. I found myself rubbing my hand across my suitcoat, just to feel my gun, just to be sure it was there. I needed the reassurance.

I tried to look relaxed, tried to stroll down the block to Briggs Boulevard. I figured I'd take a drunkard's path to McGraw's stable to be certain I wasn't being followed.

The streets were quieter than I'd yet seen them, even at night. There weren't as many pedestrians as there had been on Sunday, few shoppers, no roving summer bands of kids, little traffic except an occasional police car. Stephen O'Dell had said he'd keep the strikers home for a day or two and see what the authorities did. Apparently, he was holding to his plan, and the boomtown had almost become a ghost town.

If you'd been making a movie, if you'd have filmed the streets that morning, the emptiness of the boulevard would have been some kind of tipoff to your audience that something was about to blow up. O'Dell had wanted to blow Blind Spring so high that it landed in America, but that was no sure thing. When you blow something that high, you can never be sure where it will land, or in what shape.

I wondered if I'd be able to find O'Dell. I'd told Simpson I'd try to inform him that Chaney was heading back to town.

It occurred to me that I *was* playing a part in the strike. I had gotten sucked deeper into it than I'd intended, especially if O'Dell was right that Grant had been killed because they—*who?*—had thought he was the union organizer. I *had* ended up choosing a side.

If such was the case, at least there was no better man for me to deceive about my involvement than Anders Corman. The gray medicine man was used to deception, used to lies.

30

Four men in red neckerchiefs were leaving the stable when I walked in. Ben McGraw was standing in the back doorway, watching them hike up the steep path. John Summerset was sitting in the rocking chair by the woodstove.

"What's going on?" I asked.

"Strikers," said McGraw, walking toward me. "You saw the red bandannas, didn't you? They wear them. In the Logan County mine war, when they was arresting strikers and didn't have no charge, the sheriff just marked 'redneck' down 'side their name."

"What'd they want here?"

McGraw didn't answer for a minute or so. Looking older than usual, he limped to the front door, reached up and took his tobacco from his mouth, then hurled the wet brown wad toward the street. He took a deep, chest-swelling breath of the morning air, and turning back toward me, said, "They want the use of my farm south of town."

"Why?"

"For a camp, in case they get evicted. They're figuring it might happen, you know."

"I've heard."

"They need somewheres they can locate if they're thrown out. They got to have a place Briggs don't own where they can drop supplies. The place is near the Shawnee–Potomac line, so if they end up commandeering trains, like the strikers done in the coal wars, well, it'll work out, you see. Old Briggs'll really be cussing me now. First, I wouldn't sell him the damn farm, then I let the strikers use it."

I pictured the big head on the pillow. Wherever Timothy Briggs was right then, he certainly wasn't worried about Ben McGraw's farm. Or about the strike, for that matter.

"I already saddled your horse for you," said McGraw, stuffing a fresh plug of tobacco in his mouth.

"You ready to go?" asked John Summerset, rising from the rocking chair.

"Yeah."

"Best go out the back way and across the hill, like the miners done," said McGraw. "They say there's mine guards posted on the corner below the company houses. They could stop you, and if they recognize Summerset here, they might haul him in on general principle."

I followed the whiskey man out the rear door, over the small bridge, and up the rocky trail. No baskets of bootleg were slung over the back of his horse this morning, and it was the first time I'd seen him in clear light. He struck me as even bonier and more wizened than I'd thought.

At the top of the hill, he picked up speed, riding the ridge like he knew every side trail in western Murry County, which he probably did.

"I guess Suze filled you in on all the details when she and Moses came to see you," I said, catching up with him.

"We should have thought about Harry before, but we didn't. I suppose we figured no one from Blind Spring would have much to do with Philadelphia people. But there was ones who benefitted, of course. Harry'd be one of them. He always was mean, someone you didn't want to have any truck with. I don't know if he'll talk, don't know what we'll get out of him, but it's worth a try. Anything's worth a try. You brought your gun, didn't you? I brought mine." He patted his coat pocket. "I brought along some whiskey to tempt him with, too."

"Yeah, I got the gun. Are we going to need them? Is Harry a black snake or a poison one?"

Summerset gave me a little smile to show he knew I was quoting him. "Who knows? If you want my opinion, he could have had something to do with Scott's death, now that I see how the cards were dealt at the time. You learnt more about Grant's killing?"

I decided not to tell him what Stephen O'Dell had told me about the three men in the car at the East Works. "Nothing I'd want to count on," I answered instead.

He slowed the pace as we came to the scrub forest above the company houses and started to turn right, on up the hill.

"Wait a minute," I called to him. "I have to see a guy in one of the houses."

"You in with the strikers, too?"

"Not exactly."

"Ain't no sin," said Summerset.

We rode to the edge of the hill above the miners' homes. I climbed down from the horse and, a bit unsure of what I was doing, moved downhill alone, pushing through the weeds and brush toward the street.

On each small porch sat a red neckerchiefed miner. They were biding their time, watching the same bunch of kids play ball in the steeply sloped street. Now and then, one of the strikers would look down to the bottom of the slope, where a black car blocked the intersection and a group of mine guards stood around.

When he saw me emerge from the bushes, Kayce Powell got up and made his way through the ballplayers.

"How's it going?" I asked.

"Quiet, so far, just like O'Dell said it would be. Except you can tell they're hemming us in, like we're in jail or something."

"There's been talk they may evict you."

"I heard."

"I wanted O'Dell to know what I learned this morning. Fred Chaney could be back in town at any minute. Briggs wired him first thing. Looks like they're waiting for Chaney before they make a move."

"Figures," said Kayce. "I'll tell O'Dell when I see him. He's going door-to-door right now, giving pep talks. Anything else on your mind?"

"No. . . . Well, yeah."

"What?"

Some deep seam impulse made me ram my hand into my pocket and pull out Grant's wallet.

"What's this?" asked Kayce when I handed it to him.

"Just take it."

He opened the leather. "I can't take this. There's a lot of money in here."

"You can use it. If the strike lasts a while, if you people get put out on the street, you'll need it. Buy something"—I stopped myself from saying, Buy something lacy for Polly—she wasn't Clair Bascomb, and a striker's camp was no dollhouse—"Buy something to make life easier on everyone, easier for the kids, the baby, the babies."

"Where'd it come from?" he asked.

"It's Frank Grant's. He's not about to complain. O'Dell knows what Grant was like. Besides, you saved us the other night. At least, you saved me. If they'd found the two of us in this neighborhood, both of us would have probably ended up dead."

I turned away and started up the hill before he could argue about it. Hell, not only would Grant, with his tales of railroad battles and strikes, have approved of the donation, but the

Mazzillos had told me some of the money used to hire us came from miners who'd wanted to see justice served. Well, let the money come full circle. They could use it.

When I got back to the horses, John Summerset was sprinkling tobacco on a cigarette paper. He licked the paper, lit his cigarette, and asked, "You finally all set?"

He was halfway in the saddle before I could answer. "Black snake or poison, we'll find out," he said, his face screwing up so its lines curved in all directions as he blew out smoke.

31

"Briggs and Company'll find a way to get back at Ben McGraw for letting the strikers use his homeplace, won't they?" I asked.

"The bastards always find a way," responded Summerset, resignation in his voice. "But there's more folks than Ben hates them. Why do you think I'm on this errand with you?"

"Is this how you'd get up to the East Works, too?"

"Yeah. We got to be careful, quiet, from here on. They probably got guards along the road to the mine making sure there's no vandalism."

He came to a halt and seemed to put all his police-avoidance skills to work before rapidly leading me across the road into a narrow lane. His business had made him a careful man.

"What are you going to do if you find Harry had something to do with murdering Scott?" he asked as we rode between the trees shading the way.

"I don't know. Ask Chaney to arrest him?"

"You think he's going to admit Alberto Gatini didn't do it?"

"Every question's new to me. I've never been here before."

"You better figure it out. You're here now."

We rounded a kink in the lane and a field opened up before

us. It looked as if it hadn't been farmed for years. Through the high grass, I could see a cabin ahead of us.

It was too rambling a place to call a cabin, but, in its present condition, it was shy of what you'd call a house. The old log structure looked like no one had worried with repairs for ages, and the outbuildings had either all caved-in or been dismantled for firewood.

We left our horses by a pile of boards with an axe stuck in one, and started for the cabin. I was glad I wasn't making the visit alone.

The door was half-open. From the crooked way it was hanging on its rusty hinges, I wasn't sure the thing ever closed properly. Cobwebs were strung across the top of the doorframe. The windows were cracked and broken in various degrees, and some of them were covered with dirty newspaper.

"Harry! Harry!" called the whiskey man.

When there was no answer, we ventured in.

"Ain't much of a housekeeper, is he?" said Summerset.

"Understatement."

It was hard to judge whether the smell was worse than the chaos that greeted our eyes. A chair, one leg busted off, was tilted sideways in the middle of the trash-littered floor. Insects crawled over the leftover food on the dusty table. In the afternoon heat, something smelled terribly rotten.

Summerset studied the stuff on the table and picked up an empty canning jar.

"Your brand?" I asked.

He nodded. "Harry wasn't exactly putting up beans last night. You either sell brew to people like him, or you don't. He ain't going to allow himself to run dry."

"I'm not preaching at you. I just asked."

Summerset put the jar back down on the table and looked around, taking in the ruins. He walked through the front room toward an inside doorway. Suddenly, he stopped cold.

"We won't get nothing out of Harry today."

Harry Mays was lying on his face on the floor next to his bed. If I had been him, I'd have slept on the floor rather than on the filthy mattress, too. Stretched out like he was, he was bigger than he'd appeared shuffling down the company house hill, and it occurred to me that he must have been a powerful man before he'd become so ravaged. Certainly big enough to wield an axe, I thought, suddenly remembering the axe at the woodpile. Now, however, flies were using his heavy gray coat as a landing field. Next to his mouth was a pool of pinkish vomit. Next to his hand was another whiskey jar.

Summerset knelt beside Mays. "You ain't getting nothing out of Harry *any* day. He ain't breathing."

I squatted beside him. The sickening odor from the body was powerful.

"He ain't been dead too long," said Summerset, touching the drunk's clawed-up hand.

I picked up the canning jar. There was still half an inch of whiskey in it. I took a whiff. "This your stuff? Does it smell right?"

The whiskey man took the jar from me, tilted it toward his nose, and sniffed. "They might say it's mine, but it ain't. I never sold nothing like that." He held the jar up to the light coming through a jagged window. "I'd say it ain't just bad whiskey. What if it's been poisoned?"

"You mean intentionally?"

"I mean someone could have put poison in it, that's what I mean. They could take a jar like I use and put poisoned whiskey in it. Harry was probably too drunk to notice. The old son of a bitch would drink anything you give him."

"Who would have done it?"

"How the hell do I know? You're the detective, ain't you? I didn't see him last night, but he buys from anyone. He either got this from some fellow he trusted, or someone brought it here special for him, which is more likely the truth."

"That sounds right."

"Who knew we was coming here today?"

"Only you, me, McGraw, Suze, and Moses."

"We're all clean. No one else knew? You didn't tip anybody off any way?"

I ran back through everyone I'd seen since meeting Suze at McGraw's stable late Monday afternoon. Stephen O'Dell, Simpson, Clair on the phone, a delirious Timothy Briggs, Dr. Corman.

"Corman. Christ."

"What?" asked Summerset.

"There was one person I might have tipped off. Briggs' doctor, Anders Corman." *Big medicine man.* "I got in an argument with him this morning. You see, he's the one who bought the land for the East and West Works before Briggs moved in."

"So he's the one would have had some tie with Harry Mays."

"Yeah. I'm afraid so. I guess I'm the reason Harry's dead."

"I'll take that as a confession," said someone—someone who wasn't the whiskey man or me.

I swiveled on my knee to see Josh Kirk standing in the doorway behind us. The chief deputy had a pistol pointed our way. "Stand up and lift your hands over your heads," he ordered.

"We didn't have anything to do with this," I said, climbing to my feet.

"That's for a jury to decide."

"A jury like the one convicted the Italian?" said Summerset.

"I'm not getting in no debate with two killers," said Kirk. "Come out of there slow, and keep those hands up." He kept the gun on us as he backed into the main room.

I noticed that John Summerset still had the whiskey jar in his hand as we moved from the room.

Kirk noticed, too. "That's a prime piece of evidence there.

Glad I got here before you wiped your fingerprints clean, or removed it altogether. I assume you boys came back here to be sure Harry drank the stuff you left for him."

"We didn't poison it, and we didn't leave it for him," I said.

"He knows that damn well," said Summerset, staring angrily at Kirk. "You're the one, ain't you? You brought the jar up here earlier. What'd you do? Put some dope in some brew you confiscated one night? You afraid you'd lose your high deputy badge if Harry talked to us?"

"Everyone says you're the one who actually solved Scott's murder," I said. "You're the one who picked out Gatini as the stooge, to lay the rumors to rest."

"Some detective," barked Kirk. He was losing his manners.

"Who told you I was a detective? Anders Corman? Did he give you the poison and send you up here this morning?"

"I could shoot you two with good cause right now," said Kirk, his face reddening with each word. "I could say you resisted arrest. I could say—"

Summerset hurled the jar at Kirk, but the deputy must have seen it coming. He ducked out of the way and then fired before the whiskey man could get his own gun out of his pocket. By the time Kirk turned his attention toward me, I was ready.

He looked surprised, Kirk did.

I pulled off a shot before he could react. I'd never killed a man before, but it was easy enough.

As easy as shooting Moses' pasteboard target.

Kirk's gun thudded on the floor and he staggered backward, exhaling a dull yell, as if all the air had been punctured out of him. His hands went to cover the hole in his chest and blood poured between his fingers. He tried to get away—tried to make it through the doorway—but collapsed just outside.

I leaned down to check on John Summerset. He was unmistakably dead. I stepped outside and looked down at Kirk. I was pretty sure he was dead, too.

Then I heard the car.

The motor roared and the driver tore down the lane as fast as he could.

With his last ounce of energy, Kirk had tried to get outside. Who was he trying to signal? Not Chaney, if he was back in town, or Smithers, or some other cop. They'd have been right on top of me. In fact, they'd never have let him enter the cabin alone once they'd seen the horses outside. No, it was someone who wouldn't want to get involved in a shootout, but someone who could drum up more mine guards.

It was time to get away.

I holstered my gun and stared down again at Kirk's body, at what I had done. *Thou shalt not kill.* What commandment wasn't I going to break in Blind Spring?

There was no sense trying to cover anything up. Just leave the bodies where they lay. Summerset, Mays, Kirk. One blown away by me, the other two dead because of me.

Just ride away. But where the hell would I ride? Where could I find a safe place, a safe house?

Not the Briggs Hotel. Not McGraw's stable for any length of time. Not the company houses surrounded by cops. Not the Mazzillo bakery—God, the whole building would quake.

I only had two choices—the two women, Suze Chester and Clair Bascomb. And Clair had called me, had wanted me to come to her, had wanted to tell me something.

I hoped I'd have enough time to get to her, and then up to Suze's, before the mine guards closed in.

32

Confused and upset by what I'd just been through, it took me a while to find Clair's by the cross-country route. Eventually, by chance as much as any innate sense of direction, I landed at 117 Dutters Drive. The street was quiet and empty, and seemed a thousand miles away from the cabin now stuffed with corpses.

I had second thoughts about leaving the horse out front. I might as well tack up a sign announcing my presence. So, I opened the gate and went through Clair's flower garden, leading the horse behind the yellow house, where I tied it to the fence in a spot I didn't think could be seen from the road.

I'd started walking back toward the front when the kitchen door opened.

"You can come in this way," she said. "Is something wrong? Why did you tie your horse out there?"

"I . . . I don't know. Just thought it was a good place to leave it. No, nothing's wrong."

"You look like you need a drink. Come inside."

She was wearing a floor-length Oriental robe, and the red silk seemed to shimmy, the golden dragon on her back was breathing flames, as she led me through the kitchen, then through the small dining area, past the half-closed sliding panels, and into the bright red parlor she was so proud of.

She pointed to the chair next to the red sofa. "Sit down. I'll be right back with something to relax you."

I sure needed something to relax me. I sank into the plushness of the chair and tried to get my head clear. I wasn't going to be much good if I couldn't think straight.

When she returned, Clair was carrying a tray with two glasses. She placed it on the long coffee table and sat on the couch. The golden dragon on her back rested against the pillows at the far end of the sofa.

Clair reached forward for one of the glasses, and her red robe slid open. Beneath it, she was wearing a short black shift just like the one she'd worn for the photograph on the wall behind her. The photograph, her in person—it was like seeing her twice, like seeing her in stereoscope.

She swung her bare ivory legs up onto the couch and softly said, "Go on. Have your drink."

I leaned over and picked up the glass. My lips were already touching it when I smelled the smell—the same smell I'd noticed in the whiskey jar at Harry Mays' cabin.

"What's the matter?" she asked, squirming around on the sofa until her black chemise was almost up to her waist.

She jumped when I threw the glass. It smashed into the photograph, sending splinters of glass flying and knocking the picture off the red wall.

With a harsh edge to her voice, she demanded, "What are you doing? You're as crazy as *Junior*!"

"You're not going to poison me," I said, pushing myself up out of the chair.

"Sit down," said a man.

Dr. Anders Corman was standing in the doorway to the foyer. He was wearing the same gray pinstriped suit he had that morning in the *District of Columbia,* except now he had a revolver in his hand.

"It would have been much simpler if you'd only swallowed the whiskey like a good boy," he said.

"I'm not Socrates. I don't die on command."

"Oh, a little knowledge," said Corman. "You talk so tough for a college boy. Don't you think I know the police are after you for killing Josh Kirk and, I imagine, the old drunk, too? I assume you have a pistol under your coat. I'd appreciate it if you'd remove it with your left hand, lay it on the coffee table, and go over and sit in the chair by the window where I can see you better."

"What are my other choices?"

"You no longer have any. We offered you choices. We gave you the chance to work for us, but you turned us down. Now, I either shoot you, or you do as I say."

I didn't know what Grant would have done. Hell, he might have lifted out his gun and, daringly, thrown it at Corman or something. Of course, John Summerset had already been killed for trying a similar trick. So, I pulled out the gun, dropped it on the coffee table as instructed, and moved over to the chair at the front window.

"Bring me the gun," Corman told Clair.

After she handed it to him, he put it in his pocket and gave her a quick glance. "Go call the sheriff's office. Chaney should be back in town by now. Tell him his beloved Deputy Kirk has been shot, and we've got the murderer here."

Once she'd left the room, I asked, "Where's your car? You were the one who went to Mays' place with Kirk, weren't you? You had to be. You guys wanted to make sure the drunk had downed the whiskey you gave him this morning. You must have acted fast. You had to have called Kirk just after I left Timothy Briggs' room."

"The car?" Corman laughed. "You were careful to tie your horse behind the house, boy. I'm not stupid either. Of course I act fast. You're the one who doesn't know what he's doing. You're the one who blurted out your theory about me, my brother, and what could have happened five years ago. You don't seem to understand. The prospector's killer has been tried and convicted by a jury. I was home in Philadelphia during the entire trial. As far as Harry Mays goes, he simply bought a bad batch of whiskey. The stuff's all over town. Why, you almost drank some yourself."

Clair came back and sat on the arm of the couch, her silk robe open to display her body. "The sheriff's on his way," she told Corman.

"You two have been working together all along, haven't you?" I said. "You called her this morning after I told you I'm a detective. That's why she invited me over this afternoon. I bet you even arranged our Sunday session, after I'd left Junior's room on Saturday night. You just couldn't figure out why Grant and I had really come to Blind Spring, could you?"

"Your enlightenment was a bit slow," responded Corman, waving the gun around as he talked. "No one's going to believe any of these conspiracy theories, least of all Fred Chaney and Timothy Briggs. Chaney's merely going to consider the fact you killed his favorite deputy. To believe you, the bastard would have to admit the wop didn't murder the prospector."

I found myself laughing.

"What's so funny?" asked Clair.

"You people. You really hate each other, just like Chaney told me. No one trusts anyone else." I stared over at her. "Your boss here, the mad doctor, made a wise investment in you, didn't he? You're even cheaper than all the land he bought and sold. He knew Jim Briggs' fancies, as you put it. He knew you'd see a lot of adorable Junior and be able to keep track of what the Briggs family was doing while he was back in Philadelphia. I bet he even figured you'd keep tabs on Chaney. The doctor knew the sheriff's fancies, too. Trouble was, after your first tryst with Gentleman Fred, you'd have nothing further to do with him at any price. He must have scared you bad."

"You're so silly, so naive," said Clair, glancing past me out the window.

I started on Corman. "When she refused to keep seeing Chaney, you put Josh Kirk on your payroll, right? He kept you informed about Chaney, and you used him to plant the idea in the sheriff's head about the Italian murdering Scott. You didn't want any paths leading back to Harry Mays. Did you hire him to axe the prospector, or did you just offer to pay Mays a few more dollars for his land if he cleared the way for the Happersalk property? I'm sure Harry didn't cost much, did he? You must have hated to see him return to town. When I tipped you off that I knew about the deeds and about him, you and Kirk came up with the poisoned whiskey. I guess I did you a favor. You don't have to worry about Harry anymore, and you'd have had to get rid of Kirk one way or another, wouldn't you? What will you do with Clair?"

"What's he mean, Andy?"

"He doesn't know what he's talking about," Corman told her.

"Junior was smarter than you gave him credit for, wasn't he? Took him a couple years, but he finally caught on about Clair. That's why he had his outburst on Saturday night. That's why you convinced the old man to send him back to Philadelphia."

"He knows everything," said Clair.

"He's just trying to set you against me," said Corman.

"Aren't we going away? Aren't we getting out of this scummy town?" she asked him.

"Of course, we are. Only a few more days and we'll be taking a Western tour like the President. We're nearly finished here."

A car pulled up out front. I watched through the window as Fred Chaney and his henchman Smithers started up the walk.

Soon, Chaney's bulk stirred the hot air as he pushed into the room. Smithers, scowling as usual, tailed behind him. Clair pulled her red robe closed when she felt the sheriff's eyes on her.

"What's happened? You say Josh is dead?" asked Chaney, his gaze switching from Clair to me to Corman's gun.

Corman proceeded to pour out the lies. He gave the sheriff a story about Clair calling him because she wasn't feeling well, but when he'd arrived, I'd been there, rampaging around like Jim Briggs at his craziest. He pointed to the broken glass on the floor.

Corman then said he'd tried to calm me down, but suddenly I'd begun rambling about having just shot Josh Kirk at a wino's shack, and it didn't make any sense to him, but he thought Chaney might want to look into it.

Corman's story didn't make much sense either, but Fred Chaney looked like he believed it, or wanted to.

"That's exactly what happened," said Clair when Corman was done. She must have wanted that Western trip awfully bad.

Corman pointed at me. "He'll tell you all sorts of things, Fred. He says he's a detective. The boy's deranged. He belongs in the state mental hospital at Weston, if you want my professional opinion. We may never completely understand why he murdered Deputy Kirk. Such a shame, such a personable young man on the surface, but so sick underneath. He even believes this drunk, Harry Mays, was the man who killed the prospector back in 1918."

"Not the wop?" asked Chaney, giving me a strange look. Corman had read him right.

"You may want this, Fred," said Corman, reaching into his pocket and producing my gun. "Apparently, it's the weapon he used to shoot Deputy Kirk."

"I *am* a detective," I said. "Grant and I were sent here to find out who murdered Scott. Everything the doctor says is a lie,

Sheriff. You'll find Kirk's body at Harry Mays' place. You'll find John Summerset's, too. He was killed by Kirk. And there's Mays' body. He was poisoned by your chief deputy, who was blindsiding you, working on the sly for the doctor here. It was important for them to pin the prospector's death on Alberto Gatini because Mays did the axing. Five years ago, when you were away in the war, Corman convinced Mays that the only way he'd buy his property was if he could buy Charlie Happersalk's too, but Scott had a deal with Happersalk and wouldn't even talk about selling the rights. After Timothy Briggs came to town, everyone just assumed he was behind it all, not Corman. When Briggs told you to reopen the case last summer, Corman couldn't afford to have the truth come out, so he had Kirk frame Gatini."

"Listen to that. He is crazy, ain't he, Doc?" said Chaney, stuffing my gun in his pocket.

I glanced at Smithers, who looked bored by my speech. He was staring down at his watch, like he was timing me, like he had somewhere better to be.

"You'll also find Edmonson believes Timothy, or you, or I, had something to do with the death of his buddy Grant," Corman told Chaney.

"Christ. We'll take care of him from here."

"I'm sure you will, Sheriff."

I was sure they would, too, and I didn't know what the hell I could do to stop them.

33

Smithers' pistol was pointed at my back when I walked out of Clair Bascomb's house and moved toward the black car in front. The handcuffs dug into my wrists, making me feel a little like Alberto Gatini must have felt being led to slaughter on Thursday morning.

"Let's take him down to the jail," said Fred Chaney as soon as we were in the car. Smithers steered away from Dutters Drive, and Chaney stretched his arm along the top of the front seat. His fist was clinched.

"Hell," he moaned. "Go away for a day, and look what happens. Goddamn miners go out on strike, and a crazy boy runs around pretending he's a detective and kills Josh." He tilted his head so he could keep an eye on me in the back seat. "Would have saved both of us a lot of heartache if you'd gone away when I warned you, Edmonson."

"I know you don't believe me, but I told you the truth," I said. "The detective agency will raise hell over me getting framed." At least I hoped they would.

"I don't want to hear it," Chaney snarled.

Smithers drove past the well-guarded Briggs Hotel, turned right at Briggs Boulevard, and rolled past the strike-deadened storefronts. When I saw the time on a clock, I couldn't believe it. Talk about losing time on a ferris wheel and gaining time on a bad day. It was only three o'clock. The three hours since I'd stepped into McGraw's stable to meet the whiskey man had been the longest three hours of my life.

Smithers turned again, toward the sheriff's office. I'd never been arrested before, and wondered if they'd give me a chance to contact the agency and let the boss know I was locked up. All my hopes, it seemed, were pinned on some faraway salvation.

"What'll we do now?" mumbled Chaney, just before we reached the office. "Shit, Smithers. Let's take this boy up to Harry Mays' cabin and see for ourself what happened."

Smithers steered past the jail and maneuvered the car up a side street and crosstown toward the company houses. We stopped at the roadblock below the miners' homes. Chaney said something to the deputies stationed there, then turned back to me again. "Squat down low. I don't need the asshole strikers seeing you with me."

Lying across the floorboards, I couldn't see the red-neckerchiefed strikers on their porches as we ascended the street, but I could hear them, even with the windows rolled up. The men sprayed the auto with curses. Then we were past them, and I was past any chance of help from Stephen O'Dell, Kayce Powell, or any of the others.

"You're going to wish you was one of them damned miners instead of being whoever the hell you are," said Chaney, wiping the sweat from his forehead.

The sweat was running on me, too, as Smithers pulled in at Mays' lane. We bounced our way over the ruts between the row of trees and the deputy drove the car across the field and right up to the cabin door. Summerset's horse was still tied near the pile of lumber.

Chaney hopped out and hurried over to Kirk's body. Smithers held his gun on me as I climbed from the back seat. I guess I could have kicked at him and run, but I wouldn't have gotten fifteen feet.

"So you did this?" Chaney sneered as we approached. "We don't need nothing more on you, boy, as far as I'm concerned."

"It was self-defense," I said. "He came in while Summerset and I were studying Mays' body. He shot Summerset and turned on me. I told you how he and Corman were working together, what it was all about."

"I didn't believe you back at the whore's house, and I don't believe you now," said Chaney, so worked up that spit flew with his words.

He stepped over Kirk's body and went inside the cabin. I followed, with Smithers close behind. The place smelled ten times worse than it had a couple hot hours earlier. The stench was enough to knock you down.

Chaney looked at the whiskey man's body on the floor beside the kitchen table. Then he moved to the back room and peered in at Mays'.

"How'd the moonshiner get into this?" asked Chaney.

"He was a friend of Scott's, and he knew the drunk."

Chaney twisted around to look at me. "We should just plug you here and put out the news you all died in a shootout. You and that damn professor, why'd you have to come to my town?"

"We've been through all that."

"He deserved what he got, whether he was a communist organizer or not. I got no regrets that Kirk and me give the bastard a good workover, dropped him in the coal car, and shoveled coal on top of him. We don't have to go to so much trouble with Edmonson though, do we, Smithers?"

"Guess not," said the deputy.

"I thought Timothy Briggs gave all the orders," I said. "Wasn't he the one who told you to get rid of Grant? He called you back to town last Thursday night, didn't he?"

"I'm the sheriff," answered Chaney. "I make my own decisions. I get the credit, like I did with capturing the wop. The old man don't know everything. The union man had him spooked, and he didn't want to have to worry about him. That's all he told me. Kirk and me was out on patrol that night and found your professor snooping around town in the middle of the night, so we figured he was the one. I'm still not so goddamned sure the pair of you wasn't sent here by the UMW. The whole shebang about Scott and Mays could just be to embarrass Mr. Briggs and Blind Spring at a hard time."

"Is there a good time to embarrass you guys?"

"Boy, I wouldn't be so damn smart-ass. We're through talking." He started toward the cabin door. "Shoot him, Smithers. Let's save the legal papers and the cost of a trial. Let's get out of this graveyard."

When I heard Smithers cock his pistol, I considered rushing at him to try to knock the weapon from his hand. That's not how it worked out.

"Turn around, Sheriff," said Smithers.

"Shoot him! What is this?" asked Chaney. He was every bit as surprised as I was to find the gun pointed at him. "You two working together?"

If we were, I was sorry I hadn't known it all along.

"You're under arrest for the murder of Frank Grant, and probably for some other things," said Smithers.

"You're arresting me?" bellowed Fred Chaney. "You can't arrest me! Not in this town."

"Like hell, I can't. Take out your gun, drop it on the floor, and kick it over this way," Smithers calmly ordered. "Then, take Edmonson's gun out of your pocket and do the same."

"I'm going to walk out this door and forget you ever said that," said Chaney.

The bullet split into the door, a foot from the sheriff's beefy shoulder.

"I don't understand," whined Chaney.

"The governor sent me here. He got a letter from a woman on the mountain telling him that Alberto Gatini couldn't have killed Lancelot Scott. He also got complaints from the railroad about the way you manhandle passengers at the station."

I remembered then. Suze Chester had said she'd sent the governor a letter. She'd said she'd never gotten an answer. Now, she had.

"I thought you was thrown off the state police," said Chaney.

"That's what you were supposed to think."

Hell, Smithers sure had had a better cover than the one about Grant and me being folklorists.

"Christ, Smithers, we can work this out," insisted Chaney, taking a new tack. "Let's get rid of Edmonson. I'll make you chief deputy to replace Kirk, and we'll go see Mr. Briggs. He'll pay you better than the state does. He'll reward your loyalty. You could end up with a downtown block, like I got the bakery building. Use your brains. You'll never pull off putting me in my own jail."

Mercifully for me, Smithers ignored the bribe. "Any minute now," he said, "a train loaded with state troopers will show up at the station. Just drop the gun, Chaney."

The sheriff wasn't giving up easy—he had more guts than I'd figured. But when Smithers pulled the trigger again and the bullet nearly brushed his coat sleeve, Chaney jumped. Then he dropped the pistol to the rotting floor and kicked it toward the state trooper.

"Pick it up," Smithers told me.

I bent down to get the gun, and it was then I lost track of what was going on. Smithers began shooting, and when I looked up, I saw Chaney with my gun in his hand, his finger on the trigger. He was wobbling backward, his shirtfront liquid red. The revolver fell from his palm as he dropped in the doorway, almost across Josh Kirk.

"Ends that son of a bitch," said Smithers.

Lose your railroad, lose your wife, think you're great?

"I don't know what I'd have done if you hadn't changed sides," I said.

Smithers kicked the gun away from Chaney's hand. "I never changed sides."

"I thought you were the worst of the bunch, a renegade blackleg who pushed little guys off the station platform and followed me around."

"I had to make myself look like the worst so they'd trust me fast. I tailed you because I didn't want anything to happen to you. When you lost me at McGraw's stable, I figured you could take care of yourself better than you looked. Turns out you could—until today. You figured out the whole tangle about Corman, Mays, and Scott. I was leaning that way, but couldn't fit all the pieces."

"You were such a bad-ass that the whiskey man and some of the other people you needed to befriend wouldn't come near you. So you knew I was a detective all along?"

Smithers undid the cuffs from my wrists. "I didn't know till after Grant was murdered and your boss wired the governor. I figured Chaney and Kirk had slugged Grant around, but I couldn't prove it. The two of them probably had all sorts of secrets between them."

"The three of them."

"What?"

"Kirk would have told Corman everything."

"Yeah, well, anyway, I kept waiting for evidence, but, when the strike started, I couldn't wait any longer. There was no future in letting the mine guards bash in heads and giving Chaney the reason and chance to bump off more people. This morning, I contacted the governor and asked him to send in state police."

He reached down, picked up my gun, and handed it to

me. "You may need this." He took a step toward the door, then stopped and looked down at Chaney and Kirk. "You got one, I got one, I guess. We share the credit, and the blame."

Smithers' eyes weren't yellow at all, I noticed. They were as brown as mine.

34

As we drove to Clair Bascomb's dollhouse, I tried to tighten all the knots so Smithers was clear on how one thing tied to another. I began with the report by geologist Nate Corman and moved from there to Anders Corman, who'd come to Murry County to buy real estate cheap, but, when his plan was derailed by Scott, had somehow gotten Harry Mays to kill the prospector. Then, with Blind Spring in his mitts, Corman began selling land to Timothy Briggs to develop his empire. To protect his interests, the doctor had enlisted Clair and Kirk as spies, just as he'd tried to enlist me. If I'd signed on, I wondered, would I have ended up working for him or for Briggs?

"Greedy man," said Smithers.

"Yeah, but then Grant got killed, and it doesn't seem like Corman had anything to do with it. If we believe Chaney, old Briggs didn't have much to do with it, either."

"It's all still greed, no matter how you look at it. It's in the air, and Corman and Briggs pump out the air."

Smithers pulled the car into a small road about a quarter of a mile from 117 Dutters Drive. We climbed out and walked the rest of the way on foot. The sun was slanting west, creating a perfect mess of glare and shadows through the trees and bushes as we sneaked toward the house.

We came at the place from the side. Smithers crept up and peeked through a parlor window. The red room was empty, and he slipped the window open as quietly as he could. Guns in hand, we climbed in and looked around. No one appeared to be downstairs.

We went into the foyer and started up the stairs. A step creaked once and I was sure they'd heard us, but they must have been too busy.

They were at the vanity when Smithers pushed open the bedroom door. Clair's red robe was on the floor near Corman's coat and pants. She was bent forward at the waist, her black chemise hiked up high, and Corman, still wearing his white shirt and tie, had entered her from behind. He was moaning, "Now, now," and she was cooing, "Andy, Andy." They were so entranced with watching the mirror image of themselves going at it that they didn't notice Smithers and me at first.

"Shame to interrupt this tender moment," said Smithers, half-laughing as he stepped into the room.

After Clair and Corman were uncoupled, we used Smithers' handcuffs to hook the doctor to a post of the bed. If we'd have thought to bring Chaney's cuffs, we could have locked her up, too. As it was, she simply sat on her vanity chair moping, her delicate fingers playing with a lipstick.

"Shoot them if they budge," Smithers instructed me. "I'm going down to call the sheriff's office. The state should have moved in by now."

"The state?" asked Corman as Smithers left the bedroom.

"You don't want to hear it," I told him.

Clair turned toward me and pointed at Corman. "He made me do everything. I wanted to tell you. He used to visit me in Philadelphia, and he offered to set me up here. I really didn't do anything wrong."

Corman shot a stare at her but didn't bother to open his mouth. Instead, he sat on the edge of her bed with one wrist cuffed to the post, his free hand rubbing his gray temple, his cock hanging down between his shirttails.

"I didn't know the whiskey I gave you was poisoned," Clair told me. "He gave it to me. It must have been something he had in his black bag. He promised me I wouldn't have to do anything except let him know who was in town and what was on their minds."

"It's always different beneath the surface, isn't it?" I said.

She recognized her own words. "Shit," she said, turning her back to me and staring into the mirror.

"I see we're all still warm and cozy," said Smithers when he returned. "A couple troopers are on the way. We'll turn this little party into a real gang-bang."

"Troopers?" asked the doctor.

Smithers picked up Corman's pants and tossed them on the bed. "You'll feel better about being arrested for Mays' murder if your ass isn't showing when you walk into the jail."

Clair grabbed her red robe off the floor. As she slid into it, she gave Smithers the line she'd tried to feed me. "I didn't do anything."

"You and the doctor will be charged with attempting to murder one Bill Edmonson," Smithers announced. "Prostitution's against the law, too. You'll love jail, Miss Bascomb. We'll have to put you in solitary, you understand, to keep the men away from you. We'll post a jailer outside your cell at all times to be certain you're safe."

"You've got nothing on me," said Clair, pulling her robe tighter around her body.

All the makeup in the world couldn't have covered up the hatred on her face.

35

"Delightful girl," said Smithers as we watched the state cops lead Clair and Anders Corman down the walk to one of the late Fred Chaney's black cars.

I felt as if things were out of my control now, as if I wasn't part of it any longer, as if I were watching a motion picture, one directed by the master, D. W. Griffith.

Clair looked out the window at us as the car pulled away. She had the same vicious expression on her face that she'd worn upstairs. And then her face was replaced in the movie by Corman's. Over and over again, Corman's. First, the dapper gent who'd chatted with Grant and me on the train. Then the "concerned" physician in Junior's hotel room on Saturday night. Then the angered speculator in Briggs Senior's room that very morning. Finally, the man pointing a gun at me in Miss Bascomb's red parlor. All the same man, but different all the same.

Suddenly, it was Briggs I was seeing. The big head on the pillow. The big head attached to the withered body.

You almost had to feel sorry for the old man. His miners were on strike. His sheriff and chief deputy were dead, shot while trying to kill Smithers and me. His town had been invaded by state troopers. His son had been shipped away in disgrace. His friend, the gray doctor, had betrayed him on several counts. His reputation was as wrecked as his health, and now his drugged mind was rambling through some tangled forest.

I turned to Smithers. "What happens now?"

"Well, you can go, as far as I'm concerned. Just leave me an address where I can reach you. They won't indict Corman until the Murry County grand jury convenes in September. The girl will crack by then. She won't take a rap for him. We'll charge him with poisoning the drunk and trying to poison you, and with bribing a deputy sheriff, Josh Kirk. I don't know it's possible to get him for murdering Lancelot Scott, even if he was the one behind it."

"What happens with old Briggs?"

Smithers chuckled. "I suppose I'll go see him in the morning, just so he knows he's not exactly in charge anymore. I'll call in his whole damn police force—all his mine guards—and take their deputy badges away. They should never have been deputized in the first place. We'll pack the worst of them out of town in a boxcar and deposit them in downtown Pittsburgh or somewhere."

"So, they won't be moving in to evict the strikers?" I asked, thinking of Kayce Powell and the other red-necked strikers on their nervous lookout.

"That's what Sheriff Chaney was plotting when he got back to Blind Spring. He was planning it when we got the call to come up here to the girl's. But I won't help Briggs evict anyone." Smithers stared at me, serious. "My father is a coal miner."

"And the strike?"

"That's the old man's problem, not mine."

"How about Gatini?"

"The way I understand it, the governor already has pardon papers on his desk, ready to sign. He's just waiting for a signal."

"Good."

"This your first case?"

"Yeah."

"You didn't screw up too bad. Who hired you and Grant to clear Gatini, anyway?"

"I . . . I can't say."

"I figured as much. Look, I'll be going down to the jail. Do you want a ride back to the hotel?"

"No. I've got a horse in the backyard, and I've got some people to see."

We shook hands, and Smithers hiked down the street toward the car we'd hidden. I headed around the dollhouse to the horse, trying to get straight in my head how I'd tell the tale to the Mazzillo clan.

With the son translating for Papa Mazzillo, it took nearly two hours to make it through the saga. They were smothering me with thanks by the time I finally got away from their house.

The sun was diving in the west, but I knew I still had to ride up into the mountains, up the old dug road to Suze Chester's. At least I could spend the night at her place and not have to worry about getting back to the Briggs Hotel.

Scott's photograph sat on the kitchen table, his eyes gazing out at me as I filled Suze in on all the details. Moses sat across from me, straining to understand everything as best he could.

When I was through, Suze picked up the picture of Scott in his tam at his crude mine, his hole in the mountain. Looking at him, she shook her head. "I'm sorry about John Summerset," she said. "I always told Scott none of it was worth it. Men die in the mines all the time, and they die to own the mines. They die for all sorts of no good reasons, don't they?"

36

The Shawnee–Potomac eastbound squealed out of Blind Spring a minute or two behind schedule on Friday morning, June 29, 1923. Waving goodbye from the platform were Suze Chester, Ben McGraw, and Moses.

The station had been quieter than I'd ever seen it. Despite the strike, despite all that had happened in the last week, the platform looked like a railroad platform anywhere. Smithers was doing his best.

This time, as the train meandered its way through the Mountain State toward Maryland, the scenery wasn't blotted out by a cloudy night, and I saw what I'd missed when I'd come with Grant. We roared past leafy mountain jungles, between steep shale cuts, into dark tunnels, then back out into sunlight.

It felt strange to be disconnecting from the boomtown, strange to simply ride away from a place where I'd been so enmeshed, where I felt as if my life had changed, strange to ride away free and alone and alive.

Where have you been, Lord Randal, my son?

It had been my first case and I wasn't so sure. Nor could I know the events that would soon happen, and how those events would cause me to think back on what I'd been through.

I couldn't know that Timothy Briggs would slip over the line within a week, that Simpson would find him dead one morning in his bed in his hotel. Or that by early December, when I would return to Murry County for what they called the Corman-Bascomb Trial, Briggs Junior would be sitting at a bargaining table with Stephen O'Dell and a delegation of miners. His old man would really have occasion to harp about Junior's weakness.

I couldn't know that President Warren G. Harding, like Frank Grant, wouldn't come home from the journey he'd begun on June 20, that Harding would die, somewhat mysteriously in August, after railroading down the coast from Alaska to San Francisco. Or that Calvin Coolidge, who believed, like Timothy Briggs, that the business of America is business, would soon be President.

I couldn't know that Grant had pegged it right when he'd predicted an all-New York World Series and no batting title for Ty Cobb. Or that one October day I'd be sitting in the stands when the Giants' Casey Stengel, not the Yankees' slugger Babe Ruth, hit a home run in the opening game.

Hell, I couldn't even know whether I'd stay a detective. Or, if I did, whether I'd end up flat-footed and dog-eared or not.

During the District of Columbia layover, I walked the same sidewalks I'd once walked with Grant, and I ate in the same greasy spoon. Back in Union Station, I bought a *Washington Star*, but the events in Blind Spring weren't mentioned. In fact, they never made the New York newspapers, either. Outside of Murry County, it was like no one knew what had happened.

There was nothing in *The Star* that I was in the mood to read, so I tossed the thing on the bench and fell into watching people come and go, like dignitaries in a newsreel. I couldn't help noticing the pretty girl sitting across from me. I tried to talk myself into starting a conversation with her. Couldn't hurt, I told myself. Adventure and women—life could be a whole lot worse.

You could end up a wealthy old bastard in a hotel bed, just a big head on a pillow, with no one left to listen to you. Or you could wind up dead on the floor of a lousy cabin, shot by a crooked cop. Or you could be crushed in a coal car. *They die for all sorts of no good reasons, don't they?*

Turned out the girl was from Alexandria, Virginia, and she was waiting for the same train I was. She was heading north to spend the summer with her great-aunt. She planned to return to the university to study literature in the fall.

"I'm something of a literature student myself," I told her. "I'm on my way back from West Virginia where I've been researching folklore, old songs and stories, you know."

"Really?" She sure sounded like she was interested.

I nodded nonchalantly. "Have you studied Child's ballads in your classes?"

Grant's goddamn line had to be good for something.